Treading on Borrowed Time

by
Evelyn Klebert

Treading on Borrowed Time
By Evelyn Klebert
A Cornerstone Book

Published by Cornerstone Book Publishers
Copyright © 2010, 2019, & 2024 by Evelyn Klebert

Interior Art Include Images by Evelyn Klebert

First Cornerstone Edition - 2010
Second Cornerstone Edition – 2019
Third Cornerstone Edition – 2024

Cornerstone Book Publishers
Hot Springs Village, AR
www.cornerstonepublishers.com

ISBN: 978-1-61342-214-4

Dedication

For my husband,
my true love, my best friend, my hero,
and my deepest inspiration

"But He Who Dares Not Grasp the Thorn, Should Never Crave
the Rose" – Anne Bronte

Table of Contents

Treading on Borrowed Time

The Old Man on St. Anne's Street

Chapter One

It was difficult listening to the murmurs around her. She concentrated, trying to shut them out. Perhaps it was a mistake to come out today. But it was the first sunny day in so long, and the heavy weight of the camera strap around her neck reminded her that she hoped to get pictures.

Her head throbbed a bit, but she hadn't eaten much for breakfast — not the smartest move for an insulin-dependent diabetic. But she couldn't be bothered by it, not today, not while other things were pulling her. She kept drifting down Decatur Street. It was a Saturday morning, close to summer, the end of May, and the French Quarter was buzzing with activity. She'd parked at Jack's Brewery but had no specific destination in mind. So, she turned onto Madison Street, not pausing to question, simply following the flow of energy.

It was disconcerting what he felt — a distinctive presence, one that felt connected to previous lifetimes. Christian Montamat strode with purpose out of the front lobby of the Royal Orleans Hotel into the heart of New Orleans' French Quarter. There was business to deal with — business for which he had traveled from his homeland of England. He stepped outside into the warm, humid morning. The thickness of the air hit him palpably, as did the acute wave of agitation from the street ahead. He deliberately turned a corner, moving away from Bourbon Street.

As he crossed to Conti and began a trek toward the river, the rush of anxiety subsided. Clearly, there was too much humanity in turmoil in that area, and he didn't need the distraction. Attempting to clear his mind, he focused on the task at hand, but again, the awareness surged up—the familiarity that tantalized him, compelled him. Someone else was walking these streets today, someone he'd known long ago.

Whispers egged her on. She reached into the pocket of her blue jeans, pulled out a mint, and popped it into her mouth. Hopefully, the quick sugar would hold off the inevitable plummet for a bit longer. She had no business being out here today in the heat. She loved New Orleans. It was home, but the summer weather, and for all intents and purposes, it was summer now, was brutal, and she couldn't even think about the pile of work waiting for her back home. Being a freelance commercial artist was an ongoing tap dance of deadlines, juggling, and canvassing for work.

It was a toss-up to say whether she was indeed an artist or just a slave to the public's vacillating tastes. But this was another consideration that would not be settled today.

Her feet led her to a quick left turn and then a right onto St. Ann's Street. It certainly wasn't an area she frequented, nor was the Quarter, for that matter. She lived in a small wood frame house off of City Park Avenue that had been left to her by her parents. They'd died nearly five years before in a car crash. And having no siblings, they'd left her an orphan, and she still felt like an orphan at twenty-nine.

She paused, speculatively, before she continued. Compared to the busy, crowded streets she'd walked along earlier, it was odd how remarkably deserted St. Ann's was. There were only one or two people and an eerie quiet that felt entirely out of step with the franticness of the rest of the Quarter in its weekend crush. A draft swept down the lonely street. She scanned for its other occupants she'd seen moments before. The woman had disappeared, perhaps into a doorway or down a connecting street. But the man was still there, across the road about half a block away. She slowly continued her trek, noting even the cars parked along the way were few and far between. Glancing to the side again, she saw that the man had not moved. He was an elderly fellow but dressed strangely, unseasonably warm for this weather — wearing an ill-fitting tweed suit and a nearly matching sloping hat perched across his white hair.

Again, a cool breeze coming out of nowhere swept down the street, running a curious chill up her spine. Perhaps it was her blood sugar out of sync, but truly, chills weren't her usual symptoms.

She now stood directly across from him, feeling drawn to inspect the curious figure. Hopefully, it wouldn't be interpreted as some sort of rudeness. But he hadn't stirred from his spot. He remained motionless, his back a bit stooped from age and needing the support of a cane.

Perhaps it was foolish, but it wouldn't be the first foolish thing she'd ever done. She crossed over to him until she stood in the middle of St. Ann's Street, staring directly into the old man's eyes. It was as she suspected. She saw fear and confusion. "Have you lost your way?" she asked quietly.

He glanced about furtively and then nodded. There were tears in his eyes as she felt his confusion and pain pass into her.

Perhaps the heat of the day or her blood sugar threatening to plummet had caused her to misinterpret the situation. What was clear was that this poor lost soul was a wandering spirit—a ghost, if you will—because, among other things, Julia Moreau could see the dead.

"What does it look like?"

"Clear like the air, but dense, reverberating, focusing energy."

"Where can I find it?"

"It travels, merges, but must always end up near the water — turbulent, living waters."

"Is it bigger than a bread box?"

The channeler's eyes flickered open, piercing into his with deep gray orbs. "Are you not taking our guidance seriously?"

Christian frowned. It bothered him to be forced to seek outside help. He was not without his sensitivities. In fact, his own psychic powers were formidable, but oddly enough, in this very important matter, he seemed somewhat blocked. "No, no, believe me. I'm taking your guidance extremely seriously. It's just not too specific."

Again, the eyes widened. The woman's counsel he'd sought came highly recommended. She was in her late seventies, well established as a medium but clearly as eccentric as the electric blue fringed sarong in which she had draped herself. Unfortunately, Christian did not have the temperament to tread lightly where egos were concerned. "I can only impart the information that is given." And then the gray eyes narrowed, "It seems deliberately non-specific. This conductor you seek is shrouded by old magics."

"Really?" he straightened up in the uncomfortable antique wooden chair he'd been perched upon for the last fifteen minutes of her non-specific session. "Old magics?"

She accented her nod with a dramatic hand swirling in the air that nearly always seemed to accompany her dialogue. "And there's more."

He waited, then impatiently prodded, "More?"

Again, she nodded, and her hand swirled in earnestness this time. "Yes, it will be through another that you will gain what you seek."

He felt a curious flux of energy as he turned off Royal Street. A quick rush of awareness surged toward him — again with the familiarity so strong. Then he remembered the words of Maxine Dupres, nearly six months before, during his visit to France — "It will be through another that you will gain what you seek."

And unexpectedly, he suddenly noted that the street he'd turned onto was deserted. All the areas he'd traveled in the French Quarter that morning thus far had been literally crammed with people but not this one.

He moved to the center of the road and closed his eyes. The draw was intensely strong — somewhere here definitely, perhaps somehow lodged between realities. He cleared his mind, willing it to strip away layers of obstruction, and then slowly opened his eyes again.

The scene before him had changed quite a bit. A cold breeze swept down the street and, dare he say, whistled. And there was activity. People were meandering slowly, window shopping, dressed less casually, in coats and winter wear from a different time, perhaps fifty or sixty years before.

A dizziness passed over him. There was a different time layered here. And then he spotted the oddity, some three or four blocks down — a woman, a young woman dressed in a light cotton blouse and blue jeans, clearly out of place. As he walked forward, the air became denser, thicker, and more difficult to move in. Clearly, he wouldn't be able to sustain here very long. It was misty, but he could see her ahead of him. She stood in the street like himself but stopped, speaking to someone. Again, it hit him, the intense familiarity. She was the focal point and foolish, so very foolish.

He didn't even have to concentrate on her aura to see the energy just bleeding out of her, giving it her all, clearly at great expense. His steps reached a quick stride as he moved to catch up with her.

It was an aunt, a great aunt, who first began appearing to her in the house at Solomon Place. Julia's marriage had broken up several months after her parent's car accident. The marriage that her mother had warned her emphatically was a mistake. What was it again that her Great Aunt Lilia had told her. *"It clearly was your path, my dear. That was why you wouldn't hear anyone."*

"But it was such a mistake."

"You really shouldn't be quite so judgmental, my dear. We plot our lives to learn, and sometimes, the very best places to learn are in difficult situations."

It was odd in reflection. She'd married just out of college, and the only way she could describe it was like being in a fugue. It was a strange fog where she was somehow locked in with blind determination that seemed unfathomable now. All the signs and distant warnings going off in her head went un-heeded. *Everyone else must be wrong.* What a shock when the fog lifted so quickly after the honeymoon and reality set in. And the rest of the story became about trying to make do with something that wasn't right.

Julia took a deep breath. It was so easy to get sidetracked in this place where she was, somewhere between — somewhere hidden deep in this poor lost soul's reality. Her aunt, her long-deceased Great Aunt Lilia, had first appeared to her at Solomon Place, so odd to remember. It was after her parent's death. After their death, after the divorce, she fell into a hole, a dark gray shrouded place of depression. She could feel it now, the tantalizing feelings of despair trying to wrap around her like tentacles — his or mine, she wondered, or both? The old man stared at her with frightened eyes. *"You must understand they are clinging so hard to the life they once knew. But the more they resist what is, the more warped their reality becomes. It becomes a nightmarish landscape. First, you must comfort them."*

She smiled at him even though she was shivering. It was so cold here on the plane where he existed. "It's all right. I'm a friend." His eyes widened. Most of the people he encountered probably never acknowledged him. How could they? He was a spirit just living on the physical plane.

He shook his head in negation. He didn't trust her. *"They must be guided to move on."* How exactly would that happen if he didn't trust her at all?

Dizziness swept through her. She was exerting too much here. That was clear. "You must move on," she stated as emphatically as she could muster. "You must move into the light."

"Demon, devil," the old man muttered under his breath. "Women, the scourge of the earth." His frightened eyes had suddenly erupted in hate.

"Excuse me," she spat out with more than a bit of shock.

"This one's got more troubles than just being dead, my dear," commented a deep voice couched in a clipped British accent.

She swung around to be greeted by a tall man behind her. He had brown hair, a beard, and sparkling blue eyes. "What makes you say that?" she asked, not completely yet absorbing the fact that he was also seeing the old insulting ghost in front of her.

"It's obvious. He's off his rocker, and I'd wager it happened long before he left our world. You should be more cautious about those you choose to help."

She opened her mouth to retort in irritation at his frustratingly apt assessment of the situation when another wave of dizziness swept through her. The distracted thought that she should not have left the house without wearing her diabetic bracelet briefly crossed her mind as her surroundings crashed into darkness.

Julia's eyes flickered open to a brilliant spectrum of light — a rainbow of colors emanating from a single spot.

"It diffuses, purifies energy," she heard a voice, a voice whose source remained in shadows.

It was almost as though it lay above her head, fixed or rather anchored to something.

"It's very old, very powerful in certain hands, although it has been hidden for so long."

Her eyes drifted upward to the compelling spectrum. In fact, she felt helpless to look away. Then, abruptly, it focused on her like a beam, sending a powerful jolt of energy that was shot directly into her heart.

Julia's eyes snapped open. The stranger from the street was standing over her, and then she realized his hand was directly on her skin, on the heart area of her chest. It felt like warmth, energy pouring into her, but that did not lessen the surprise. "What are you doing?" she managed to say in a weak, croaky voice, but he seemed not even to acknowledge her.

With great effort, she pulled herself up to a sitting position, her hands supporting her on the relatively warm cement of the St. Ann Street sidewalk. She focused directly on the somewhat inappropriately placed hand the stranger had not seen fit to remove.

He still appeared to be in intense concentration, so she repeated with emphasis, breathing rather deeply. "What are you doing?" Her question pulled him from his deep focus, and he met her eyes with concern. Removing his hand, he seemed a bit dazed, as though he had been elsewhere. "I'm trying to revive you."

She scrambled awkwardly to her feet, but he was right there, warm, strong hands beneath her arms pulling her upward. "Don't rush it. You still seem ill," he murmured.

"No," she shook her head, which was still spinning. "Well, just shaky, low blood sugar."

"Diabetic?" he said with question. She nodded, still trying to get her bearings. "Well, then let's get you something to eat, Miss—"

"Julia Moreau," she obligingly filled in the awkward pause.

"Yes, let's get you something to eat, Julia Moreau. I'm Christian, Christian Montamat." And then he smiled with a charm that hadn't surfaced until now, "It's a pleasure to meet you."

Lunch With the Englishman

Chapter Two

He felt it all over her as though she'd touched it, touched the crystal he sought. His mind, however, told him how highly unlikely that was. It, the crystal as he called it, although he had no earthly idea what actual form it took, had been, for lack of a better word, created over five hundred years before by an alchemist deep in Southern France in the city of Provence. This remarkable clarifying crystal's existence was only known from the diaries of mystics. But it was not a mythology. It was real and in this city. He glanced across the table at his companion, who was quietly sipping a glass of lemonade — and this woman had somehow been near it. He could feel it as acutely on her skin as he could feel the fact that it was she whose presence he had sensed so strenuously earlier.

She glanced up as though in response to his thoughts. He smiled, trying to be reassuring, although his mind was busy calculating several steps ahead. "Feeling better?"

She had green eyes, dark green eyes framed by shoulder-length brown hair, and a delicately chiseled face reminiscent of another time that nagged at him. Striking, he had to admit, remembering what it felt like to have momentarily held her after she'd fainted. He had to remind himself of his purpose and not become side-tracked by a lovely female. "I still don't know who you are," she stated in a voice that, at the moment, sounded rather devoid of inflection.

"Christian Monta—" and he stopped in mid-sentence in response to the frown on her face.

"A bit beyond the name would be nice. What I want to know," and then she stopped as though unable to articulate her thought.

"You mean the old man."

She nodded slowly. She still seemed a bit pale. He glanced around, wondering how soon this place would get some food to them, hopefully before his lovely friend faded too much.

"Yes, how you were able—" she shifted uncomfortably. Clearly, she wasn't used to discussing this aspect of her life with anyone, "to see him?"

He took a sip of the glass of iced tea in front of him, more so to take a moment to consider than anything else. When he'd come to New Orleans to obtain this precious heirloom, he hadn't contemplated a complication of this magnitude. And yet here she was sitting before him, pale, a bit shaky, and as much an enigma as the thing he sought. "Well, I'm sure you must realize that you are not isolated in your talents."

She leaned back a bit in her chair as though contemplating this possibility for the first time. "Actually, I've never met anyone else who could see spirits as I do."

He smiled, a bit surprised, but he felt she was being genuine. "That's unusual. No one else?" she shook her head to reaffirm what he'd said. And how long have you known you had this gift?"

"Long?" she repeated. She was weak, dangerously weak, he sensed. Clearly, no one had taught her how to protect herself, how to protect her energy. "Since I was little, I would see the others — mostly the in-between ones — then for a while, I was able to block it." She glanced away.

"For a while?" he asked.

She returned her gaze to him, "Until my parents died, then everything seemed to change."

"I see," he commented. "Trauma of that sort can open certain doors."

She nodded, seeming to be very uncomfortable in talking about herself. "How about you? How long have you been able to see?"

He smiled, "All my life, I suppose. But I was trained in it. This strain of vision, if you will, consistently runs in my bloodline. It's always been a part of my life."

She stared at him speculatively as though weighing and considering his words. And then a waitress arrived with their food and for the moment her focus changed.

It's an odd feeling being a diabetic or rather having a hypoglycemic, aka low blood sugar, incident. It starts gradually, maybe a slight dizziness, then a strange slowing down of things as though you are a bit out of sync with your surroundings — detached if you will. Then sometimes there is vision phenomena — spots, blotchiness, and if severe of course blacking out.

With a plate of fried shrimp before her, Julia could feel herself reconnecting with the world again. She'd lived this life ever since she was a teenager — the constant managing of her health. It certainly wasn't anything new but only perhaps new to people who weren't used to being around her.

The man in front of her clearly wasn't diving into his food with the same abandon that she was, and that in itself made her feel a bit more awkward. But then again, for her, it went well beyond just enjoying a good meal. It was more critical, stabilizing her connection with the world around her.

There had been no time yet for her to begin to contemplate who he was, why he was here, what his presence and their bizarre interaction meant. She'd been too busy reestablishing her grip on her life functions. It was only now that these particular questions began to seriously surface in her mind.

She glanced up from the over-filled plate of food. He was watching her intently. She'd known this without even looking at him. She was now cerebrally connecting with the fact that she was having lunch with a virtual stranger, one who had pretty much seen her at her worst, and was now privy to a secret she'd kept from every other human being in her life.

Julia forced a smile onto her lips. "So, what brings you to New Orleans?"

Christian Montamat looked a bit surprised and a bit amused at the awkward nicety she'd expressed. "Well Miss Moreau—"

"Ms."

A further smile crossed his lips. "Ms. Moreau, I'm actually here on family business in pursuit of a sort of family heirloom."

"From England?"

"Yes, it dates back to the early 1600s. I've received information that leads me to believe the object in question is in the area."

She took a deep sip of her lemonade, definitely coming back to herself now. Glancing up again, she caught his eyes, his profoundly blue eyes, which never seemed to leave her face. "You're watching me closely."

"Your color is better. You seemed very ill."

It was embarrassing. She hated anyone seeing her vulnerability. "Sorry about that. I usually manage things better. It all sort of hit at once."

His expression melded into a graver one. "It wasn't just your blood sugar. The old man, you expended too much of yourself."

It was an odd feeling coming from him, as if somehow, without consciously realizing it, she'd given him leave to traipse across boundaries. "Look, Mr. Montamat."

"Given what we've been through together, you might consider calling me Christian."

She sighed deeply, "All right, Christian." She was tired. Perhaps there was some accuracy in his assessment. "I appreciate your concern. But the truth is I really don't know you."

"And this is none of my business." He finished her unspoken thought.

It was bothersome how adept he seemed at keeping her off balance. "Yes, not to be offensive, but I am none of your business."

She didn't know it was possible to frown and look amused simultaneously. But he'd accomplished just that. "Well, I feel put in my place," he delivered in a way that made her feel he was anything but that. "But you still seem a bit shaky. Why don't you finish eating while I endeavor to find a way to smooth your ruffled feathers?"

"Now look—"

He pointed to her food. "Eat, I don't want you collapsing on me again, Julia."

With exasperation, she picked up a French fry and took a bite. Tomorrow, she'd eat healthier. Today, she'd simply have to write off as being off the charts in all ways imaginable.

During their lunch, Christian worked. He worked hard to understand how the lovely Julia Moreau was a link to what he sought. Momentarily after she'd revived from her faint, he'd felt undeniably that she had been close to the Dubourg crystal. That designation was given in the journals of alchemist Claude Treme in the 1600s — a distant relative of the Dubourgs. For centuries, its existence had been rumored throughout his family, almost as if it were a legend until Treme's journals. The journals were recently obtained from his more direct descendants, who had fallen on hard times. The family, it seemed, had been willing to part with anything, even his invaluable library, for a price. So here, finally, was a chance to bring the Dubourg crystal back into his family. Its lineage descended from his mother's side, which had settled in the early 1900s just outside of Manchester.

And here he was, on its trail, a bit of a fish out of water, trying to psychically drag information out of an obstinate female. It was not exactly the journey he'd envisioned.

But she let him buy her lunch, although it was a battle. Clearly, she was suspicious. And she had allowed him to walk her to her car, but she'd refused to give him her phone number or address. So, they'd politely parted ways. He knew not to push. Trying to push Ms. Julia Moreau at this juncture probably would have been as successful as pushing that old man they'd encountered to cross over. All things must come in their proper time.

He'd decided to let her think she had things her way. Then, later, he'd track her down and unearth her connection to the crystal—all things in their proper time.

Great Aunt Lilia's Advice

Chapter Three

By the time Julia walked onto the small wooden porch at her Solomon Place address, it was late afternoon. Her clothes still felt plastered to her from the humidity and her collapse. She couldn't or wouldn't process anything yet. She simply opened the door, locked it behind, and headed upstairs to a shower — a shower, a cool drink, perhaps something to eat later. Then, she could consider what had occurred and why.

An hour or so later, now dressed in a filmy long cotton shirt over blue jean shorts, she curled up with a tall glass of iced tea in a large rattan armchair in the sunroom at the back of the house. As a child, she had played quietly here as her mother painted near the picture window on the far wall. She breathed in deeply, allowing the sounds of the fading afternoon to wrap around her. Her aunt was near. She could smell the light perfume of violets that always seemed to accompany her presence, but she hadn't appeared. For some reason, she was allowing Julia to have her space, perhaps space to reflect. This was something she couldn't seem to put off anymore as a thousand crowded impressions rushed in on her at once.

So, she did the only thing that she could. She closed her eyes, clearing her mind and allowing the thoughts to enter in their order of importance.

Again, she sat at the table of the restaurant in the French Quarter, the man — Christian Montamat in front of her, watching her, calculating with those eyes, blue like the sky, filled with depth and light, so unnerving. She'd estimated he was in his thirties, maybe late thirties, but cultured, refined but not pompously so, in a natural, more integral way. He had put her at ease in a tremendously awkward situation, which made her all the more suspicious. Why bother? Why take the time?

She focused, relaxing, and allowing herself to open up and feel what he was feeling.

She caught her breath and stopped for a moment. This wasn't the first time she'd done this. Her aunt, who ostensibly served as a guide for her, had helped her develop her empathetic capabilities. But what she was feeling here was different. Most people were easily accessible, but not now. It felt like webs, layers — prickly psychic defenses — so sticky that she felt herself getting caught within.

It was so unexpected that she pulled back enough to see herself again at the table sitting across from him, and he was just watching her — but differently now, with an unusual intensity. And then he spoke, "If you wanted to know something, you should have asked me." Julia's eyes snapped open in shock. Her heart was racing. He'd spoken to her in the present from the past.

She stood up and moved to stare out of the window into the small backyard. Her heart continued to race, "Aunt Lilia," she whispered and heard a soft rustling behind her. She turned around, not surprised to see the image of her great aunt seated in the spot she'd just vacated. She was, as she always appeared, dressed in a floor-length dark blue dress, long-sleeved, with a long row of white buttons that ran from the center of the square neckline down to the floor. Draped around her shoulders, she wore a white, almost iridescent shawl.

She was Julia's great aunt, but she always appeared as a young woman — in her middle thirties, she estimated. The first time she'd appeared, Julia had no clue who she was until she introduced herself. And that initial exchange was as much of a shock as anything. As usual, her long black hair was pulled up on her head in almost a Gibson-style coiffure. Tonight, as she looked at Julia, she definitely seemed to be frowning.

"What?" she asked with a bit of exasperation, in no mood to be criticized after the day's events.

"You need to be more prudent."

"Prudent? Care to be specific?"

"Today, with that old gentleman, it was foolish. You can't rush into a situation without first identifying what is happening."

"It was her turn to frown now. "Gentleman? Well, that was a mistake. I wasn't feeling well. I didn't recognize what he was until it was too late."

"Clearly," the spirit of her great aunt spoke through pursed lips. "And the other?"

Julia knew exactly who her aunt was referring to but had no idea how to respond. She slowly sat down on a small wicker bench positioned just near the French door leading out onto the back patio. "I don't know."

Her aunt nodded solemnly, "Yes, he is very aware."

She swallowed, "Aware?"

"Not so different from you, except he has honed his skills."

"I see," she said softly, feeling decidedly she was in way over her head. Maybe I should just back away."

Her aunt stared at her in that very strange, wise manner that always seemed a tad out of sync for a face so young. "I think it may be too late for that."

She felt more than a bit uncomfortable at that pronouncement. "Why do you say that?"

"A door has been opened, one I'm afraid you've both already stepped through."

It hummed with its own life, its own energy. It was large, the size of a dinner plate, and not unlike some strange insect — primordial that had crawled out of the earth with its fluorescent, shimmering wings of blue-green and fluttering antenna of pink shades.

"This can't be what it looks like," he muttered.

The robed figure next to him replied, "In essence but not in substance. It is elemental."

"But once it was harnessed in earth, what did it become?"

It was a monk's robes, plain gray cloth that the figure wore, but he knew him well as Gregory — an old friend from a life spent together in such a way. But now, for this lifetime, serving as his spirit guide.

"It's still shrouded," Gregory responded slowly, still trying to see. "Treme fashioned it and then disguised it."

"To what end?" he asked.

There seemed to be a slight chuckle from beneath the hood. "Because he could."

Christian woke up from a heavy, saturating sleep. He was on the hotel's fourth floor, but he could still hear activity on the street below. The city never sleeps. He mused, checking his watch. It was after one.

Sitting up in the bed, he propped himself against the wall with pillows. He was shirtless because of the heat. Even with the air conditioner, he could feel the humidity. It seemed to seep through the walls. His mind wandered again to the woman, Julia Moreau, and their brief contact earlier. It was surprising, to say the least. He'd actually felt her reach out to his mind. Her audacity amused him. But he felt more acutely that she had no earthly idea what she was doing or who she was dealing with. What was undeniable, however, even with such a fleeting contact, was the strength of her spirit and, again, the familiarity of it. If matters weren't so pressing, he would explore that avenue. But as it was—

He leaned back. He was frustrated — brick wall after brick wall. There seemed to be only one path that wasn't blocked, and it was one he did not relish taking.

He crossed his legs in a meditative fashion and held out his hands, palms up. Breathing deeply and finding that quiet altered state, he moved his spirit to travel, to enter her dreams.

It wasn't a good sleep. It was heavy, dark, encased in exhaustion. Sometimes, she found she had the power to control her dreams, and sometimes, they ran rampant in all-consuming directions. Tonight appeared to be the latter.

The sky overhead was filled with a blanket of stars, but the night was heavy and humid. The concrete beneath her feet was still warm from the heat of the day. She walked barefoot out of Jackson Square to the front of the St. Louis Cathedral, staring at its white luminescence in the moonlight. Her head spun with disorientation. She realized with distraction that she only wore a light cotton nightgown with her long brown hair strewn over her bare shoulders.

In the distance, she could hear a buzzing, like a cicada or other insect. All around her was darkness, except the moon, the stars, and the cathedral, which continued to gleam before her.

She felt the movement of the Mississippi River in the distance, even heard it, but she rationalized that it wasn't close enough to hear. But then, this was a dream, and normal conditions did not apply.

Again, the buzzing was louder now, but she didn't look for it—she could feel it in tune with her skin.

"Why are you here?" he whispered.

She didn't look to answer, just craned her neck, staring upward at the giant clock at the top of the cathedral. It was nearly 3:00 AM, a difficult time of night. But probably because of her fatigue, she had little control.

"What significance is this place?" his voice was more compelling now.

The buzzing was somewhere behind her—deep in the streets of the French Quarter, buried there. "How are you here?" she asked, now, for the first time, focusing on him beside her. He wasn't in night clothes, but a short-sleeve shirt and dark blue pants—as he'd been dressed when she first met him. She was standing in front of St. Louis Cathedral in the middle of the night, dressed in a nightgown.

Then, suddenly, it changed. Her head swirled, and she walked along a long gallery outside an enormous house — the river not so far now. It was loud in her ears, and she felt its restlessness in her veins. And he sat there, someone she knew. He sat in a wooden rocking chair, staring out into the heavy night, waiting for her, as though he'd done it a million times before — hand outstretched but different, a different face.

"Is it near?" She was brought back to the cathedral again, facing Christian with puzzlement. This was so odd, disconnected from the usual flow of dreams.

"What are we talking about?"

The buzzing again grew loud in her ears. "Julia," his voice was deep and thick like the air around them. She could feel herself taking his outstretched hand, the man waiting for her, and being folded into his arms. But that wasn't now.

"Julia," he repeated, "can you help me?" And she sat up in the darkness of her room.

"Not this way," she whispered aloud.

And then, she felt a clear crystallized thought piercing through her mind. "As you wish."

Opening Doors

Chapter Four

She was thinking about Peter this morning, and perhaps that was a mistake. It was early, and she was working on a sketch for a local magazine, a pen and ink drawing of the Pontalba Apartment buildings. They made her think of Jackson Square, the cathedral, and last night's dream. The pragmatic side of her nature could tell her irrevocably that it was indeed just a dream, imbued with no more meaning than that – but her senses, her emotions, told her it was a contact. He was with her last night, and that made her think about Peter. Peter was her ex-husband, the reason that she no longer entertained romantic feelings about any man.

It is a painful place to dwell in raw disillusionment. No one can really explain to anyone else the toll that a bad marriage takes on your soul. She always thought she was stronger, stronger than most. Resilient? Smarter? And perhaps that was why warnings went unheeded. Or perhaps, as her aunt had said, it was all a path — something to learn from.

No one could have explained to her the high cost of intimacy with someone who has no real kinship with you — the price of giving someone else control of your life. It wasn't altogether, of course, but piece by piece, little by little, substituting their likes for your own, substituting their judgment for your own. It was so strange, so subtle she hadn't realized how she was being devalued in their relationship, how she began to disappear in the mighty roar of keeping him placated. She'd let her interests slip away — her drawing, painting, photography, and all of it — suppressed her psychic talents as well. By the time her aunt came along, she was shocked when she called her a sensitive, a mystic. There had been so little hint of that for so long. It had been submerged much like the rest of her. It took her some time to even realize what had happened. Almost as though you give without consent, and then they leave with a jagged piece of your soul. Then again, maybe it wasn't so for everyone. Maybe it was her nature that made the toll so high.

And all that painful baggage was making it so difficult for her to think about this man, Christian Montamat, who had intruded on her dreams last night.

Her hands hesitated above the sketch for a moment. She was working from photographs she'd taken of the Pontalba buildings, but much of it she did through vivid memory. There were pictures frozen in her mind, as was the one that had intrusively filtered in. It was a long white gallery running along the house, bare feet on its stone floor — the cool breeze from the river and the embrace of a stranger, but not a stranger. It was her, this girl in the snapshot in the long flowing gown, and it was not her. And a man was waiting, holding her, as he'd done before. She could feel his mouth on hers, still traces of the dream, her body responding, sensations. It was something she'd never known, certainly not with Peter. His touch never reached her and then, not so very long into the marriage, left her cold.

She drove the thoughts away, this odd remembrance she felt him connected to. After all, she would never see him again — the enigmatic Englishman. She sipped the hot tea she'd placed on the unoccupied edge of her art table. Just as she

24

replaced the mug and refocused on the task at hand, there was another jolt, the sound of the doorbell coming from the front of the house. She stared for a moment at the hallway, stunned, telling herself that it couldn't possibly be.

Sipping his coffee, he finished the last shreds of a croissant he ordered for breakfast. He sat in the restaurant on the ground floor of the Royal Sonesta, waiting for a call on his cell phone. The first step was directory assistance, but there was no listing for Julia Moreau. So, he contacted an old friend in Boston who was quite adept at unearthing information that other people didn't want to be unearthed. And then he'd called a car company to confirm a rental reservation. There would be a taxi downstairs for him in about twenty minutes to take him to get the car, and it would all begin.

He thought about calling first but decided the direct approach would be best. After the dream, he slept poorly the remainder of the night. He wasn't at all sure if he'd classify it as an unmitigated disaster. Perhaps he had gleaned some information, certainly some unexpected knowledge, that had nothing to do with the Dubourg crystal.

He breathed in deeply as flashes from what was clearly a past life again swept through his senses. She was young, maybe in her late teens, with long, thick black hair and a pale face but eyes — the same wide, compelling eyes. He could still feel her in his arms — the familiarity, the texture, the taste of her mouth. He hadn't lived his life outside the company of women. There had been involvements, one engagement that was mercifully broken off. But all of them had left his heart virtually untouched. He'd concluded long ago that his life path would be devoted to learning, perhaps spiritual pursuits — possibly spent like the lifetime in which he'd known Gregory. But this,

this powerful draw he felt, was unexpected and unique. Once again, he drove these more intimate impressions away.

As for the crystal, he'd mistakenly thought he could pull something useful out of her unconscious. But she was so aware. So, he was forced to take another route. As anticipated, his cell phone rang, and he answered it.

Julia was working at home today, finishing the sketch for *New Orleans Home,* and then planned to work on another layout for a local newspaper. She'd begun her day early, taking her blood sugar. Not unexpectedly, considering the chaos of the day before, it was a bit off track but corrected by a dose of insulin that she would repeat in the evening. She had dressed casually in a loose sort of lightweight, purple caftan that helped her feel the flow of energy, but it was not something she would feel comfortable receiving guests in. She moved through the long hallway in the center of the house, from which rooms fell on either side. It was a rambling, two-story wood frame house, not overly large, but it had been big enough for the small three-person Moreau family.

Of course, once her parents had died, she had no idea if she could live here at all, but when she and Peter had split up, there seemed to be little option. The two of them had resided in a townhouse he'd owned before their marriage, which remained his after the divorce. Initially, she'd considered selling the house at Solomon Place because of the memories more than anything else. But then her aunt had intervened, and within the deepness of her despair showed her that new things could grow in places that might appear barren.

She moved toward the front door, knowing it was him, while her mind told her emphatically that it could not be. To find her, he would have had to go to great lengths, but then again, hadn't he already done that?

The front door was made of a heavy red oak, and she would have to peer through a window on the side to see who had rang the doorbell. The reality was that she had no inclination to do so. She just softly rested her palms on the door, breathing lightly. She waited, wondering if whoever was really on the other side had gone, already receiving no recognition.

Her breathing was light, but her heart pounded vibrantly. She continued to wait, but there was no further response, not a knock or another doorbell ring. There was just quiet, so quiet she could walk away, and no one would know the difference.

And for the longest of moments, she considered doing just that, but something else compelled her forward — curiosity, a wildness, a thirst to fling open doors with abandon and rush outside.

She turned the lock and, without further consideration, swung open the front door. He was waiting there, perched on the porch railing, not looking surprised—in fact, not much of a reaction at all.

Julia stood in the doorframe, feeling like all the breath had left her body. "What are you doing here?" she asked.

"I need your help," was all that he answered.

Becoming the Guide

Chapter Five

Julia dressed upstairs in her bedroom, pulling on a pair of blue jeans and a long, filmy off-white blouse. The room was large and airy, with plenty of light filtering through the long beige shears. It had been her parent's room. She'd kept most of the furniture intact, including the large brass queen-sized bed she'd covered with a pale blue satin comforter. The room was decorated with light oak furniture and not cluttered with ornaments. This she had done at the instruction of her aunt. "Energy is essential. Its flow must not be obstructed." At odd times, it hit her how different this was from the townhouse she'd lived in with Peter. He gravitated to antiques, heavy, overly embellished pieces that dominated the room. Their years together had been oppressive and draining, and on reflection, she couldn't help but wonder if that décor had only served to magnify what was wrong in their relationship.

She ran a brush through her hair, trying to shake off such morbid recollections, and focused on the man waiting downstairs for her. Quickly checking her appearance in the long oval, cheval mirror, she could see that her eyes looked feverishly wide and her face flushed. Well, considering the circumstances, that seemed like a mild reaction.

He'd arrived at her door not only unexpectedly but in a strangely focused manner—not light, not charming, but as though he were carrying a considerable weight on his shoulders.

"Can I come in?" he'd asked. And she hesitated, worldly instincts telling her to close the door, but something else deep within influencing her otherwise. Her hand hesitated on the doorframe, and she looked away, completely torn and confused. It felt ridiculous in some ways, this inability to make a decision. And then she'd felt the light pressure on her hand of his covering it. Without choice, she looked up into his eyes, this stranger. They were darker today than she remembered. "I know I'm asking a lot dragging you into this, Julia, but at this point, I feel I have no other place to turn."

"How could I possibly help you?" she murmured. "We barely know each other."

And then there was a bit of a smile. "I can't pretend to understand. I can only say you have some link to what I seek."

She stared for another moment into his eyes, seeking and questioning. Then, without thought, she stepped back, allowing him to enter.

Heading down the short curving staircase back to the first floor, she drifted into the kitchen, where she'd put on a pot of fresh coffee before she'd left to change. Christian had left the room. She passed through the small paneled den where she could see him through the French doors, standing in the sunroom. It surprised her a bit. Hesitantly, she moved to the doorway, where he stood over her art table. "You really have a gift," he said, gazing back at her from her sketches. It was an awkward moment, not unlike when you've found someone reading your diary. But then again, this work would be public before too long, so she wasn't certain why it felt uncomfortable.

"Thank you," she replied. "I made some coffee. Would you like some?"

He nodded, smiling, with a bit of his smooth veneer returning, "Yes, I would."

She turned, heading back to the kitchen, not looking to see if he followed, just sensing that he was. She took two heavy white mugs that had belonged to her mother off the shelf. They were white ceramic with a raised pattern of ivy. So much of the house still bore her parents' imprint. She'd never quite let go of the feeling that this was still their house, although they had been gone for four years.

She felt movement behind her. "Do you take cream?" she asked, not turning around.

"No, just black." He'd walked away toward the breakfast nook by the large bay window. She took a moment to top her cup off with milk and a teaspoon of sugar before heading to the round table with the mugs. He wasn't seated, just standing near the window, calmly watching her.

"You seem nervous," he commented quietly.

She sat down, stirring her coffee, and then finally met his eyes. "Um, I don't know. A bit, I suppose. All of this, well, it seems a bit strange even for me."

"And you're used to being alone?"

Her eyes widened at the abrupt question. "Used to it? I don't know if that's true. I have friends. I have," and then she stopped, realizing she'd almost told him about her aunt. "I was married for a while." There was a brief look of what she could only interpret as surprise that crossed his face, and it bothered her a bit. He'd settled quietly in a chair directly across from her. "What?" she asked pointedly.

He smiled, "I don't know. I'm not trying to insult you, Julia, but you just have the aura of someone who is—how can I put this — untouched?"

She stared at him, a little stunned. "I'm not sure I understand what you mean."

He sipped his coffee, "I'm not sure I understand either."

"Well, don't you think we should talk about why you're here? This, what did you call it?"

He leaned back in the chair as though he were lost in thought. "Dubourg crystal."

"Dubourg crystal. Why is it so important to find?"

"It's very powerful and needs to be put into safekeeping."

"Why is that?" she asked slowly, already beginning to get strange and, as of yet, unidentifiable impressions floating around them.

"Well, let's just say, in the wrong hands, it could be very dangerous," he said slowly and deliberately. It was like a swirling of light somewhere, and he was watching her so closely, clearly picking up on the change. A face crossed her mind like a flicker, a man with dark hair — black like coal and eyes the same, skin so very pale. And then, in the very next instant, it was gone. "What is it, Julia? Are you feeling something?" he asked. She felt dizzy, as though the room had expanded somehow, and it surprised her.

She breathed deeply, "Light, so much light, like a prism everywhere."

He nodded, "Yes, it fractures energy, not unlike a prism."

"And I saw someone, a man with dark eyes." And she saw, in that moment, the change in Christian's face. It was a hardening of his expression. His eyes, she could almost say, became perceptively darker. "Do you have any idea who that might be?" she asked.

"Perhaps," he said slowly. What is clear is that now there is urgency?" Then he refocused on her and said directly, "Tell me about the dream."

That statement completely shifted gears within her and confirmed what she suspected. "The dream?" she asked, with a slight intonation of outrage. "What exactly gives you the right to invade my dreams?"

He frowned, "It wasn't an invasion, more of a visit."

"A visit is usually accompanied by an invitation," she said, standing up angrily from her chair.

"Calm down, please," he said softly. She hesitated, then slowly sat back down. "This is extremely important, Julia. Please tell me what you were feeling in the dream."

"I'm not sure." Another frown, clearly patience wasn't in this Englishman's repertoire. "Other than you being inexplicably there, I remember this strange buzzing sound."

"Buzzing?"

"Yes, buzzing in the distance. Then, at times, it would get stronger, like a cicada or some other insect."

"I see," he said, his expression unreadable, "that must be the crystal."

"The crystal? What does that mean? Why would some crystal make a buzzing sound as if—" Then she stopped at the thought.

"As if it were alive?"

Her eyes widened. "What are you saying? This thing is living?"

"Yes, yes, and no. It's an elemental, alive in a way we don't really comprehend. You must understand, Julia. There are so many different forms of beings just a fraction of a dimension off from us, alive surely but invisible to the eye. Some of them just exist, others feed off our energy. It's complicated. But an elemental is something extremely old, past living as we know it, but powerful."

She shook her head, "I don't really understand."

He sighed, smiling a bit, "I'm not sure that I do either, completely. But the dream, tell me, was there anything else?"

A quick flash of the woman walking outside across the plantation gallery crossed her mind, as did the man who was waiting for her. But oddly, in the moment, she decided to say nothing. It had nothing to do with the crystal. Truly, it seemed wholly unrelated. "Pretty much yes." Something flashed across his features, then he stoically began to sip his coffee again. So, is that helpful at all?"

"I'm not sure. Any idea what direction this buzzing was coming from?"

She tried to remember, although everything did seem a bit foggy now. "I think behind me, The French Quarter."

"Well, if that's all we have. Then that is where we should begin."

"We?" she asked explicitly.

"Yes, Julia, what's clear is that you are the guide."

She opened her mouth to retort, then closed it again. She had no idea what to say.

The Visit to the Cathedral

Chapter Six

It wasn't dark now but early morning, dawn nearly peeling back the layers of the evening. She stretched in her bed, trying to hang onto the feeling of peace that had blanketed her through the night. She tried to hold onto the sensation of his embrace, even though she knew it was wrong, even though she was such a young bride married to an indifferent husband. She could smell the river, feel it in her veins so close to them. It had been predicted that in only a decade, the river banks would shift so much that it would sweep past the grounds of their plantation right through the massive house itself, eroding its walls until nothing was left. She did not find it overly remarkable that she felt nothing in this regard, no affinity for the grand architecture that surrounded her. She had married into this great fortune, was mistress of all of this, and yet had never felt so isolated, so empty — except, perhaps on her wedding night, when she finally realized the harshness that would be her life. She bent her head back down to her pillow, hearing the heavy booted footfalls of her husband while desperately holding onto the last vestiges of her lover's embrace.

Julia sat up in her bed, her heart slamming against her chest. She brought her hands before her, stunned at what she felt and saw. They were trembling violently with fear. She forced herself to calm, breathing deeply — a dream, just a dream brought on by heavy emotion and exhaustion. Her eyes passed over the Big Ben clock that had been her mother's perched on the nightstand. It was just noon. She would be picked up by Christian at two. They'd agreed upon that. It was enough time for her to finish some work and rest. Her hand had stilled, but not her heart. It continued to thump painfully in her chest. She thought it must have been a dream, but it didn't feel that way. It felt acutely that for the span of a few moments, she'd been in someone else's skin.

He moved with purpose through the heavy fog, breathing the mist straight into his fiery lungs, but it did nothing to cool the intensity within him. His head pounded in response to the severity of his determination, his unrelenting focus. He was traveling at night but near dawn, and the city was largely deserted. It made it easier for him to search. He could feel the reverberations of energy, but they were muffled, hidden.

He paused in the street momentarily, and then phantoms filtered into his color-blind vision. He could feel the overlap, the people passing the street — and then another layer, the girl. It stunned him. So much that, for a moment, his concentration faltered. The recognition was intense and painful. And then, he could see him, also in her layer. And this realization was not nearly as sublime but overlaid with rage. He was already here, one step ahead.

With that awareness, he completely lost his concentration. All visions fell away as he was once again wrapped in the fog. It was clear that he was targeting the wrong time frame. He relented as pain ripped into his chest. The energy he'd spent was substantial, but it was a small price to pay for what he sought. He would rest now, then begin again.

Christian felt the shift in the air around him, in the energy, perhaps in the very earth upon which he stood. Time was running out. He checked his watch. It was one. Another hour, then he would pick up Julia Moreau and hopefully substantially narrow down the location of the crystal before— he banished the thought. He would not allow his mind to venture into certain areas. He slowly sat down in the small armchair near the window of his hotel suite. It would be dangerous to try to see with his mind. If, against all odds, he was here, it would only alert him to his presence. So, instead, as a precaution, he worked to shroud his aura in a protection or rather a disguise. And when he picked Julia up, he would work to do the same for her.

"What do you think?"

Julia waited for a response from her aunt, who was sitting quietly on the rattan chair in the sunroom. "It's difficult."

She sat down slowly across from her. "It's difficult?"

Her aunt frowned. "I have to tell you, dearest. This whole business is somewhat shrouded even from me. Just because you have crossed over doesn't mean you are all-knowing or all-seeing. It seems as though there is more than meets the eye. You must proceed with caution. These people you are dealing with are very old souls filled with light and dark. And yours is an old soul as well, entwined somehow from many lives."

"Wait a minute. What people? There is only Christian."

Her aunt's eyes widened a bit. "No, my dear, I see the three of you."

"You mean I'll meet someone else."

"No, I mean, he's already here."

It was quiet, so odd, not as expected. But what about this whole thing was expected? When Christian arrived at two to pick her up, he was charming as usual but distracted. She could feel it on her very skin. She'd made a last-minute decision to bring her camera along. In an odd way, it brought her energy, taking pictures. In a very literal way, it helped her focus. And then the drive to the French Quarter was largely silent. "Is everything all right?" she'd asked.

And he'd smiled in that remote British way of his. "Just preparing," was all he answered. She leaned back against the seat of the car and started preparing herself. Her aunt had coached her in surrounding her being with white light for protection. As she did so, her mind drifted back to their conversation. She'd asked in complete confusion, "I don't understand what you mean. I haven't met anyone else."

"That doesn't change anything."

"So, should I simply not get involved in this?"

"It's too late for that. It's karmic. You entwined yourself in this matter long ago."

"I don't understand."

"I know. There isn't much more I can say except to pay heed to your feelings and tread carefully. There is much here that is unseen."

And that was essentially all she could get out of her. Frustrating didn't even come close to what she was feeling. She was feeling something much worse, similar to what she had felt during that time with Peter. She felt that she had no control over her life, and that, more than anything, made her crazy.

"You should try to relax," he murmured as they turned off the expressway and took the Vieux Carre exit.

It jolted her a bit. She was sure he meant it as a comfort, but it felt like an invasion just now. She closed her eyes and refocused on erecting walls of protection, protection from just about anything that might come along.

It was Sunday, but Sunday afternoon in the French Quarter was just the same as a Saturday. There were people everywhere, and if she hadn't, for lack of a better word, *cloaked herself*, she would be picking up a million varying vibrations and emotions from the masses. As it was, a brief wave of dizziness passed over her but mercifully left quickly. She'd packed glucose tablets and snacks in case of another low blood sugar episode. She wasn't expecting it, but it was better to be prepared. In her mind, she hoped this whole matter with Christian Montamat would be settled today, and she could disappear again into her own life.

As they meandered down Decatur Street, still largely in silence, she knew exactly where they were heading without him speaking to her. She tried to clear her mind of all distracting impressions as they passed beside the artisans, fortunetellers, and all other manner of vendors set up along the black wrought iron fence around Jackson Square. When they finally stopped, she looked upward to the grandiose steeples of the St. Louis Cathedral. Now, he asked quietly, "All right, Julia. Where do we go from here?"

It was strange, the things that catch you in unexpected moments—just that phrase, just that intonation. Peter stood in the hallway of his condominium, staring at her with disdain, as he'd so often done near the end. *"Now Julia, where do we go from here?"* So odd, the undetected poisons that the past pours in at inopportune moments.

She closed her eyes in response and let her mind travel back to the dream, back to the darkness all around. "Can you hear it?" Christian's voice, but was it from the dream or now?

In a wave, realities began to tear and separate like thin tissue paper. She could hear it behind her, behind her back — the sounds, the buzzing, the elemental. *"Julia,"* she could hear her name again, but who was calling? Then she felt a massive crackling of the air all around her, followed on its heels by a violent, nearly physical punch in her spine that caused her to lurch backward in a spasm. There was a loud roar in her ears, then more pain, physical pain everywhere, as the air around her was ripped, and she was forcibly yanked into another place.

Christian stood in front of the St. Louis Cathedral, staring up at the huge clock centered just below its central steeple. It registered two-twenty. It was hot, and the afternoon sun beat heavily on his face. He didn't remember what day it was, Saturday or Sunday. There was an intense pressure in his head. It was Friday evening when he'd arrived in New Orleans, checking in at the Royal Sonesta on Bourbon Street. From what he could piece together from his fuzzy memory, he'd made very little progress in finding the Dubourg Crystal. In fact, the whole quest might very well turn out to be fruitless. He felt a little ill, nauseated, and decided to head back to the hotel. As he walked toward Decatur Street, something nagged at him, something he'd forgotten. But at the moment, he couldn't piece it all together. Perhaps later, perhaps after a rest. He was so caught in his own disorientation that he had no thought of the small camera bag that lay on the pavement, unclaimed, just in front of the cathedral.

The Man with the Dark Eyes

Chapter Seven

Migraines are a terrible thing. They drag you into a dark, throbbing place where everything is painful, and your only focus and the only mercy is its end. After her parents' death, Julia began to suffer from migraines. It took her about six months until she was able to rid herself of them. She had hoped forever. Of course, this was about the same time she rid herself of Peter, and the correlation did not escape her.

But this, this horrible agony, was worse than a migraine. Her entire essence felt as though it was wrapped in pain as her stomach clutched violently in nausea. She turned over in reflex. Then, someone's hand abruptly grabbed her head, directing it to a small metal pail she could barely see through squinted eyes. She couldn't think, couldn't rationalize, couldn't have one coherent thought. But once she violently and uncontrollably vomited into the pail, the nausea momentarily paused, but the pain did not. "Can you swallow anything?" The voice was deep and rough.

She felt herself panting. Did she still have a voice? She shook her head, then another spasm of pain from the movement. This was insane. Was she dying? Hands pulled her back to a lying position, but she couldn't see. The light hurt her eyes, so she kept them closed. She felt someone roughly grabbing her arm, and then a needle painfully went in. With what little energy she had, she started thrashing in objection. But the hands gripped her tightly. "Stop it. This will help. Give it a minute." The voice wasn't soothing by any stretch of the imagination. It was rough, deep, a man's voice laced heavily with frustration. "Rest," it commanded. And slowly, she felt a languidness take her over. Perhaps this was the mercy she had prayed for, perhaps not.

"It's only a matter of time."

"I suppose."

She looked outward into the night. It was cloudy overhead, no stars, just a blanket of darkness encroaching on the great house, so dense that she was sure she could feel its fingers reaching out for her. And in the distance, the rhythmic sound of the river, water she couldn't see now but feel, warm, alive, inviting. She glanced back to the French doors that led inside. She could see him in the parlor, smoking his cigar, sitting just in front of the fireplace as he did every night. Philippe wasn't an old man, by any means. He was just thirty, but he was a brittle one, unyielding, unreachable, and yes, cold.

She felt his hand briefly brush her fingers and instinctively pulled them away, turning back to her companion. He frowned. "He's just inside," she whispered.

"I must see you later."

She turned back toward the darkness, wanting in a way to disappear within it. "I don't know," she whispered. "If he finds out, he'll kill us both."

"I don't care," he answered.

She turned toward him, struck by the turbulent darkness in his eyes and knowing he spoke the truth.

Julia opened her eyes. The room was cast in shadows all around her, but even the diminished light was painful to her vision. Her head still throbbed, but not like before, not violent, just dull. As the images around her began to clear, she noted she was in completely unfamiliar surroundings. She was in a bed, an old-fashioned brass bed, in a room with light walls decorated with dark furniture. She sat up, pulling back the cover. She wore a long white cotton nightgown that, again, she did not recognize. She spun her feet around, and they touched the cool wooden floor. A sweep of dizziness passed through her mind as she tried to remember.

She was standing in front of the cathedral with Christian, just standing, and then it all became confused. Perhaps he'd brought her here. She glanced around again, trying to absorb her surroundings. There was a dresser, dark wood, not too tall, with a round mirror atop, and a small matching round table with a huge ceramic pitcher. And then, against the wall, what she could only describe as an armoire. She swallowed. Something was off. Besides the fact that she had woken up in a strange nightgown, in a strange room, something else was off. She pulled herself on wobbly legs and pushed the long rose-colored drapes aside at the window. The drapes were heavy, and a second set of light cottony type shears were beneath them. It was dark, pitch black, but she could barely make out the shadows of some kind of garden below.

"You shouldn't be up."

She clutched the drape in shock at the sound of the sudden intrusion. Slowly, she turned to the doorway, and her heart clutched for the second time in a matter of seconds. The man standing in the doorway, staring at her, was dressed in a suit, in fact, a somewhat antiquated dark grey suit, a style that clearly belonged in another time. "Where am I?" she whispered with evident fear, wondering for the first time, and perhaps belatedly, whether she should have armed herself with some kind of weapon. Her eyes flew over to the large ceramic pitcher across the room. He stepped further within, and she instinctively edged backward against the drapes. Her eyes again were mesmerized by his odd garb. She followed a long chain attached to a button which disappeared into a pocket — a pocket watch? Did anyone still use those things?

"Are you still in pain?" he asked abruptly. Her eyes met his, dark eyes which, for some reason, struck a chord of familiarity. So strange, a tall, imposing man with dark hair, longish, a beard and mustache. Again, the face reminded her of something distantly. "Do you need another injection?"

Her eyes widened, and she remembered the pain in her arm. She glanced around frantically, realizing with fully clarified import that she was really in trouble. "Where is Christian?" she asked in panic.

And then, she immediately saw and felt that this was the wrong thing to say. The eyes hardened, and a strange smirk crossed his slightly reddish lips. "Clearly, not here, Miss Moreau."

"You know my name?" her voice cracked as though it had not been used for some time.

The smirk mutated a bit into a slight smile as he crossed closer, then stopped, sitting on the bed's edge. "Yes, I don't generally pluck random women out of their surroundings without some clue as to their identity." Again, the dizziness swept over her, and a slight resurgence of nausea. "You really aren't well yet. You might want to give it some time to adjust."

"What exactly am I adjusting to?" she murmured.

He seemed to hesitate before answering. "It's complicated, and I don't think you're ready to absorb it just yet. All you need to know is that as long as you cooperate, you have nothing to fear from me. It's just that simple."

Her head spun with more than just dizziness, and a swift surge of anger at her helplessness swooped in unexpectedly. "Really? Simple, is it? What, did you just come from a costume party?"

He stood up slowly, smiling as though he were amused. "We'll talk later, Julia. I'll send Alice in to bring you something to eat." And then he headed out the door, pausing for a moment and turning back toward her. "It would be better if you didn't try to fight things. That will make the adjustment much easier." And then he was gone. She edged over back to the bed and let herself sink onto it. Some moments later, a woman appeared at the door, and Julia caught her breath again. She was evidently the maid, bearing a tray of food. She was a tall, ebony-skinned girl dressed in a sort of uniform that looked as though it came from a hundred years ago, the dark garment's hem just brushing the bottom of the floor.

He sunk into a chair by the fireplace in the study. It wasn't lit. The city was still approaching summer. That much had not changed. He breathed in deeply and felt a soreness in his ribs. This had taken so much out of him, so much energy to bring her here. It was a gamble. He recognized that. But the question was whether it would pay off. He closed his eyes, knowing that he would dream but directing the dream in an area that would be helpful to their situation.

He missed the city, the sounds, the activity, and it would not be much of a ride to return. But he could not bring himself to leave his cousin's plantation house. It had nothing, of course, to do with the house. It was an oppressive structure, filled with all the emotions of places that exploited human suffering for their own gains. But, his cousin would not view it that way. He had inherited the home from his father, and his father, and they all did business the same way. They were slaver owners. It was bred into their blood. And so, the thought that Cousin Antoine held another view would have never crossed Philippe's mind, nor would the thought that his dear cousin from the city had fallen in love with his young bride.

It was late, and he waited outside on the plantation's vast gallery to see if she would come to him tonight. It was selfish of him. He was putting her in terrible danger. He knew for a fact that Philippe considered her of no more value than anything else he possessed, and what he possessed, he would defend his right to, even if that meant destroying it. But that didn't stop Antoine. It was clear nothing would stop him. He waited in the semi-darkness, hearing soft footsteps. Finally, after a stretch of endless moments, she appeared out of the shadows dressed in a long white nightgown. Her face was as pale as the moonlight, filled with worry and indecision. She stopped in front of his chair. "I have to talk to you, Antoine. We can't go on with this. We must put an end to it before something terrible happens."

He heard her words but felt the drumming in his head, the sound of the river, of his blood like a dull roar. Nothing had awakened him to life as she had. Nothing had rallied his emotions in such a way. He stood up, grasping her and pulling her aggressively against him. "No," she whispered, but then he silenced her with his mouth against hers. It was hopeless, hopeless for both of them, but never before had he felt such hope.

Trying to Escape

Chapter Eight

His eyes snapped open. He could still feel it, the energy that he'd tapped into. And then, his awareness spread through the house. She was trying to leave.

Alice seemed like a sweet person. She was only sixteen. She and her mother worked for Mr. Burke, living in a set of rooms near the kitchen. Her elderly mother was the cook and Alice more of a housekeeper. She told Julia they had been in Mr. Burke's employ only a month. Alice was a chatty girl and more than willing to give out information. But when she'd asked why Alice wore such a strange outfit, she'd laughed indulgently, asking why it was strange. Julia gleaned from their conversation that Mr. Burke had intimated that his guest was ill, perhaps ill in the head, and might say strange things. After Julia had managed to eat a bit of soup, the young girl had helped her take what amounted to a cat bath. She'd then guided Julia back into her bed, lightly patting her hand with comfort, and whispering that she would remember things right before too long.

And then she'd left, turning out the lamp, and leaving the room in semi-darkness. But Julia did not sleep. She laid in the alien bed in the alien room with her mind finally lucid. She'd been kidnapped — an odd imprisonment to say the least. But it was clear now. And what was also clear was that not only her mental distress was a factor here but also her physical deterioration. She was a diabetic. It hadn't seemed like as much of an issue while she was ill. But now that she was eating again, no matter how little, her blood sugar would be escalating. She needed insulin in order to live.

She sat up in the bed. From what intel she'd gathered from Alice, there didn't seem to be guards about here. She could just walk out a door, wherever that might be, and escape from this bizarre place where people liked to play dress-up. She would escape, get help, and go home — simple enough. She'd seen people running about more scantily clad than in the long nightgown she wore. In fact, her current garb would be considered conservative.

Quietly, she flung back the covers and put her bare feet on the cool wooden floor. She tiptoed to the door and slowly opened it, peeking out. There was a soft light in the hallway. Her eyes caught sight of a sort of hurricane lamp mounted to the wall, but no one around. Julia took a deep breath and headed out, taking her first steps to potential freedom.

She quietly but quickly traveled down a long hallway, sparsely decorated, until she reached the top of a curving staircase. She peered down, but still there seemed to be stillness, no one about. Softly, her bare feet hit the thin wooden steps on the half spiral stairway, but gratefully she made no noise. It stopped on the threshold of several connected rooms, lined with chairs and small tables. She glanced around furtively, spotting a short hallway on the far end of the second one. Her heart began to race. Silently, she scampered across the room as she reached a heavy white wooden door with several large bolts connected to it. Her hands quickly hit the cold metal as she turned the bolt of the first and then the second. With exultation, she began to pull the heavy door open, when startlingly a hand caught it just above her and slammed it shut. He bent over her head and in a heavy whisper said, "I wouldn't advise that."

With fury, she spun around confronted by the face of what she inferred was Mr. Burke dangerously close to hers. "You can't keep me prisoner here," she rasped.

"You must be feeling better," he commented a little too calmly. She could feel his warm breath on her, and it unnerved her greatly.

"You don't understand," she said. "If you keep me here, I'll die. I need—"

He nodded, "I know, insulin. I have it. I was just waiting for you—"

She cringed against the door, aghast at the thoroughness at which he'd prepared, well, whatever he'd prepared. "What? What the hell is this? What can you possibly want from me?"

He let his hand drop, and he backed away a bit. "I would have thought you'd figured that out by now Julia. I want the Dubourg crystal."

Her eyes widened in shock. She hadn't even considered that this was about that. In fact, she hadn't had time to consider much of anything except that she had to get out. "What did you say?" she whispered.

"The elemental, it's clear you're the key."

"Who are you?" she asked, in a voice that was fading in the tumult of emotion inside her.

He felt it. She could see the concern cross his face. This kidnapper, this inexplicable costumed insane person was worried about her. He moved a bit closer holding out his hand to her. "Come with me. Come sit down, and I'll do my best to explain things to you."

She shook her head, again reaching for the lock on the door. "No, you can't keep me here. I'm leaving." And in a split second, the hand he'd held out to her moments before was now on top of hers, clasping it, stilling it from motion.

His face was so close to hers that he whispered into her completely disheveled hair, "You don't understand Julia — where you are, what will happen if you walk out that door. Chances are you'll be arrested for indecent exposure, thrown into some asylum, or accosted by some travelling brigand."

Again, she spun around to face him directly. "What are you talking about?" she rasped. "They don't do that to people these days."

He pulled his face back away from hers, so that she was looking right into his dark brown eyes. It struck her again. It was a memory, a feeling from long ago, ephemeral, and then gone just as quickly as though it was a phantom. "No, they don't where you came from."

"What does that mean?"

He pulled back completely, removing his hands from any contact with her and staring at her with an unflinching deter-mination that she found more than a bit unsettling. "There's no easy way to tell you this. My name is Nicholas Burke, and I have brought you here, to the year 1910."

She stood there, riveted to the spot, staring at him in that silent moment trying to digest his proclamation. And then she replied in the only way that she could. "You must be insane."

"Nicholas Burke."

Christian stared a bit blankly at the scene outside the win-dow of his room at the Royal Orleans. It was raining, pouring in fact, right down onto the swimming pool on the third floor that his room overlooked — a sudden, unexpected thunder-storm storm. "What did you say?" he asked quietly. Moments before he had returned a phone call to his assistant in

Manchester. He had acquired enough real estate and business holdings long ago that he'd hired someone to help manage his affairs.

"I said there were two calls early in the week from a Nicholas Burke. He said it was important that he contact you. Of course, I didn't give out your whereabouts."

Christian sunk into the chair beside the window. He'd booked a flight earlier that morning to leave New Orleans. After visiting several antique shops and museums in the area, it was clear to him that his search for the Dubourg crystal wasn't going anywhere. His head throbbed decidedly as he tried to absorb Clarice's words. "Burke," he repeated.

"Yes, he said that the matter would keep, and oh yes he sends his regards." Christian swallowed on a dry throat.

"Good enough," he said abruptly, ending the conversation on his cell phone. It was Burke, Dr. Nicholas Burke, who had nearly purchased the Treme papers from right under his nose in Florence. His blood chilled a bit as he recalled their first meeting at his home outside of Manchester just a month after he'd acquired the documents. It was a rainy day, not unlike this one. And Burke was dressed in a raincoat over a dark suit. He wasn't an old man, perhaps late thirties, near his own age. But there was something distinctive about him. It wasn't often that he'd taken an immediate dislike to someone, but this Nicholas Burke elicited a nearly violent aversion within him. It was nothing in particular that he could pinpoint. He'd been pleasant, even polished for an American.

The meeting itself hadn't lasted long. They'd only sat for a few moments in his study, and as he remembered Nicholas Burke was particularly direct. "I'm not going to be in England very long Mr. Montamat, so I'll get to the point." He'd listened quietly, wishing in that moment that he'd arranged to meet him elsewhere, anywhere else in fact rather than his own home. "I'm interested in buying Claude Treme's journals from you."

"Really, do you realize I just obtained them at a substantial cost?"

"I do," he said abruptly. "It seems my negotiations for them fell through." And then he'd smiled coldly, he thought in memory, "You trumped my price."

"Well, that is the nature of negotiation."

He nodded, "Indeed, so I won't waste your time. I'll offer you double what you paid for the Treme papers."

He shifted in his chair. The man was hungry for them. That was the only way he could describe it. "That's quite an offer, considering their cost. But I'll have to decline. This goes deeper than business. It is a family matter."

And then he remembered a darkness pass over his features, something repressed, something that looked perhaps distantly like rage. "Yes, I can understand when there are personal connections involved. But you see, I understand more than you think."

It was odd that moment — odd then and odd now that he'd forgotten it. It was quite subtle. There was a pulling sensation seeping into his brain from his eyes. Christian's mind had become clouded, and he'd felt it, almost like fingers prying into his thoughts, looking, prodding. Immediately, he used his own training and pulled back abruptly. A slight smile traveled across the other man's face. "You won't get what you want that way Burke," he said standing abruptly. "I think it's time for you to leave." And then Nicholas Burke responded with no resistance, standing up as well.

Without a word, he turned and walked to the door to exit the study but then had paused on the threshold for just a moment. "Perhaps not," he responded. "But mark my words, I will get what I want."

He looked out again at the rain. The name Burke had surfaced many times in his quest for the crystal. Everyone he approached, even Maxine Dupres in France, made reference to the dark-haired American who had touched base with her. It was unclear, unclear as to whether Burke was shadowing him or several steps ahead. He'd had him investigated rather thoroughly, a psychiatrist, a background in parapsychology, and then his travels literally all over the world from what he could glean, studying and mastering esoteric doctrine. All of this explained his obsession with the crystal — a powerhouse of esoteric energy.

He breathed deeply, trying to calm himself, and eradicate the fogginess that seemed to have clung to him for days now. It bothered him, immensely. Something was wrong. Something was missing. He sat there working, trying to clear his mind with meditation, but he encountered walls or rather shrouds covering the truth. He stood up and walked back to the desk where he'd let his cell phone drop after the conversation with Clarice. The first call he made was back to the airline to cancel his flight.

Adjusting to Life in 1910

Chapter Nine

She sat in front of an unlit fireplace in a small comfortable room lined with bookshelves and antique tables, old paintings, and ceramic ornamentation. And she told herself quietly that they were not in 1910, that this was just a house decorated with an old-fashioned flair. She shivered, although it was nearly balmy. That much had not changed, the weather was consistent. And then she stopped her train of thought. She would not accept this lunacy. He took a light beige throw that looked intricately woven that was draped on a nearby rocking chair and handed it to her. Begrudgingly, she wrapped it around her shoulders. "Would you like a brandy?" he asked.

"Sure," she muttered. "It will probably send my blood sugar through the roof, but with all this stress I'm sure that has happened anyway. So, bring it on." Silently, he handed her a glass he had poured moments before. He settled in a chair directly across from hers. "You know, Mr. Burke, not that I accept any of this, but people with diabetes in 1910 would basically just waste away and die. There were no insulin treatments until—"

"1912," he finished for her. "Yes, I know Julia. But in case you don't remember, I also told you I have insulin, syringes, and a blood glucometer."

"I don't use syringes," she said softly. "I use the pens."

"Well, I can give you the injections if—"

"Like hell!" she spat out. "I've experienced your injections." And then she stopped herself. "This is crazy. We aren't in 1910. I can go down to the pharmacy and get insulin, and you're out of your mind."

He sighed deeply, sipping his own brandy. "You really should calm down as you said it's not good for you." She abruptly put the glass down on the small round table beside her and stood up. He didn't stir, just eyed her calmly. "Sit down Julia," he said in a low, methodic tone. "If you calm down and clear your mind, I will attempt to explain things to you." She hesitated — something about his tone. She didn't want to do anything he asked, but she did want to get out of this situation. Maybe if she humored him, maybe made him believe that she accepted things, then he would let down his guard. Slowly, she sat back down, collecting her thoughts.

"You must realize Mr. —"

"Nicholas."

"Um, all right, Nicholas, you must understand how upsetting this is, well, to me."

"Of course," he replied smoothly.

"And I don't know why you think I can help you with this thing you're after. But I can't. I have no idea where it might be."

"Yes, that's understood. But you do have gifts Julia."

Her eyes widened in surprise. How did he know this? How did he know so much about her? "I'm not sure what you're referring to."

"You see spirits. You feel energy, perhaps feel others' emotions."

"How do you know that?" she whispered.

Again, he sipped his brandy. "I am not without my own abilities. That is how I brought you here. Time is not a linear thing. It flows with ebbs and curves like a river, and sometimes bends back upon itself."

"I don't understand," she murmured, feeling a bit lulled by just the sound of his voice.

"Its fluidness can be taken advantage of. What is clear is that the elemental came to the city during this time frame. It came here, before it settled into its hiding."

"What do you mean hiding?"

His voice was so soft, and she could feel it closer now, nearly in her mind. "I don't know why it's linked to you. But it is drawn to your life force."

"You speak as though it's alive."

"Yes Julia, it is very much that, very much alive." It was frightening what she saw in his face. He believed all of this, but then again so had, and the image of Christian flooded through her mind. He was with her at the cathedral, next to her. If she had just disappeared as this man suggested, he would know. He would be looking for her. "No Julia," he stated quietly. "I'm afraid he won't be."

Her eyes narrowed at his impromptu assessment. "He won't be? How did you?" and then she paused, struck by a more disturbing new horror. "Are you reading my thoughts?"

He leaned his head back in the rocking chair he occupied, closing his eyes. "Not exactly, reading images, you'd be surprised how many people actually think in images rather than words. So much easier to grasp their intent quickly than transcribing sentences. No, Christian will not be riding on a white horse to rescue you, no matter how appealing that may sound. That is even if he could find you."

"You know him?"

He straightened up and opened his dark eyes, strangely eyes the color of the brandy in her glass. "In a circumspect way, I know him. We seek the same thing."

"What? This crystal thing?"

"No Julia, power, simply power."

Her head spun again in dizziness, "I can't help you with this."

"I'm sure you can't see it now. But you will, but you really must rest. The transition, the journey, so to speak took a great deal out of you. More than I anticipated and for that I apologize. You should take your blood sugar and then retire. In the morning, I will outline our agenda."

She frowned, "Our agenda? You assume I've decided to cooperate."

"Well, you want to go home, and I want the elemental. Give me what I want, and I will do the same."

Her breath caught. He made it seem so simple, made something she felt to be impossible so simple. She glanced away and then impulsively picked up the glass of brandy and took a sip. "I don't understand how you know me."

She could feel his dark eyes on her, intently watching her every move. But she didn't look at him, instead looked down at the brandy glass that she held in her hands. "You," he said a bit softly, "actually were unexpected. I was tracking the crystal, keeping my eye on Christian as he was following the same path and—"

His voice trailed off. She glanced up in a bit of surprise at the change of his tone. "And?" she asked pointedly.

"And I found all of the sudden that he was making progress. The energies had shifted. What was secure was no longer, frankly because of you."

"I don't understand any of this," she said pointedly.

He shrugged, "You don't have to understand. Sometimes life simply thrusts things upon you, when you have a role to play. In India, they call it karma, unfinished business from past lives. People's lives are intertwined for inexplicable reasons to them but linked in the grand scheme of things."

"You make it sound as though all this has nothing to do with you, as though you had no choice. This whole situation is of your own making."

He just stared at her for a moment intensely, in a way that sent chills up her spine. "Perhaps," he commented slowly. And then he put his glass down on the table beside him standing up. "You really should get some rest. Tomorrow we get to work." Slowly, she stood up as well, wrapping the lacey ecru-colored throw tightly around her shoulders. "Do you want to check your blood sugar tonight?"

She shook her head, feeling another sweep of disorientation sweep in. "No, I'll wait."

"Very well, in the morning then. There are also a few things that you should know. I had to make some explanation of your presence to the staff, Alice and her mother Jessamine. So, I explained that you were ill, recovering from a fever, and," he hesitated, "and that you are my wife."

She took in a sharp breath, not at all sure if she'd heard correctly. "You what!"

"It was the only practical solution. There is a certain decorum in this time that we lack in our modern age. It wouldn't have been acceptable for a woman like yourself to be living under the roof of a bachelor. We, of course, have separate quarters given your illness."

"Do you have any idea how outrageous all of this is?"

"Well, then we better get to work quickly, so you can have the life you want back." His words fell on her coldly. The life that she wanted? He motioned for her to precede him out of the room, and she began the more somber walk this time back to the spiral staircase.

Nicholas lay down in the small single bed in his own room at the opposite end of the hallway from Julia. He'd escorted her silently back to her room. She still seemed ill to him or, at the least, off-balance. And he took total responsibility for that, his actions bringing her here. It was one thing taking such risks himself but quite another dragging, and he hesitated on the description, an innocent into the mix.

She'd seemed lost in thought, when he bid her good night, thoughts that were hidden from him. She was more difficult to read than he'd anticipated. She was also more vibrant, more intelligent, more gifted. He sighed deeply, more beautiful and more vexing than he had anticipated, more of everything.

When he'd left her in her room, sitting on the edge of the bed, she'd given him a parting glance — eyes wide and filled with distress. It was something he should have anticipated, given what had occurred, but he hadn't expected it to tear at him so much. He'd removed his coat and jacket and just lay on the bed, still half dressed in exhaustion. He had to recharge, regroup. What was clear was that the fog he had created in Christian's mind would not last. It would only be a matter of time before he was on their trail.

Navigating a New Era

Chapter Ten

Julia tried to close her eyes, but her mind was spinning. How in the world did she get pulled into this situation? But then she remembered her aunt, her dear aunt, and her words that there were three of them.

Instinctively, her eyes opened as she detected the familiar fragrance of violets she connected to her Aunt Lilia, and the shadows across the room mutated into a familiar figure. Tears streamed down her face in response to the most welcome presence. She nearly sprung out of the bed and walked over to her and, at that moment, dearly wished that she could throw her arms around her. "Aunt Lilia," she nearly sputtered out in a loud whisper. "Oh God, can you help me get out of this?"

She smiled comfortingly, "Calm down, my young one. You need to keep a clear mind."

She shook her head frantically, "I can't. This man, he's out of his mind."

Again, she smiled serenely, as though nothing in the least was amiss. "Come, let's sit down, Julia, and talk."

Her aunt perched on the side of the bed, and Julia, frowning a bit, sat beside her. It bothered her how calm she seemed, given everything that was occurring. "Can you help me get out of here?"

Her aunt looked at her solemnly and replied softly, "No."

"That's it? No?"

"It's just more complicated than you think."

"Well, let's see. I've been kidnapped by a madman who, at any moment, could decide to come in here and vivisect me. And all you can say is NO?"

Her Aunt Lilia looked at her pensively. "He's a very determined man, single-minded, and brusque, I should say."

"Brusque, isn't that polite? He's a lunatic. He told me we were in 1910."

She smiled sadly, "Yes, I know. That's part of what makes things so complicated."

"That he thinks—"

"No, my dear, that you are. You are in 1910. Nicholas Burke has achieved a sort of time-bending. You are in 1910."

Her words hit her like a punch in the stomach. She'd dallied with the idea, but it couldn't be, couldn't really be. "Impossible."

"No, dear, it's not impossible. Remember the old man on St. Ann's Street. He existed in a different time plateau."

"That was different. He was a ghost."

"Yes and no, the world operates differently than the way most conceive it. The past is not solid. It is fluid and adaptable and can be touched by the present and the future. Everything is so tightly woven, so tightly connected."

She shook her head in denial. "It doesn't make sense. You couldn't even be here, Aunt Lilia. You're still alive."

She smiled kindly, "You're still stuck in linear thought, my dear. Where I am, you can travel to all time frames, to all past lives, so many places you can't conceive. But it's the life you're living now that you must be concerned with."

She sighed with deep disappointment, "He wants something I can't give him. I don't know how to find this thing."

"You must use your gifts, your feelings. That's the only way."

"I don't know if I should help him. Why is he so obsessed?"

She frowned, "There are always hidden things that drive us, that perhaps we don't even acknowledge. It's complicated. But you are the only one who must feel what to do."

"I'm so frightened," she whispered.

"I know," she said, her voice so comforting. "But I will stay with you until you fall asleep."

"No."

"No, Miss, it won't look right."

"I don't care."

"But it's the proper fashion. Otherwise, the dress will droop."

"Then it's going to droop."

Alice stood back, hands on her hips, staring at Julia in disdain. Julia wore a long navy-blue tailored dress with tiny white ruffles lining the waist and neckline. She had endured the plethora of undergarments required for the ridiculously elaborate outfit and the short white gloves and matching navy blue hat that made her feel like she was trying to emulate the English monarchy. But she refused, with no compunction, the small bustle that would add an uncanny dimension to the outfit. Granted, it was a slight bustle. Evidently, the fashion was transitioning, but she was determined to make at least this small leap into the future. "It just doesn't look right, Mrs. Burke."

She grimaced. How that title grated on her nerves. But she smiled with the greatest amount of charm that she could muster because, after all, it wasn't this girl's fault that her employer was a lunatic, a kidnapper, and, evidently, from what her aunt had confirmed, a time traveler. The sweet girl wasn't privy to any of this. "Thank you, Alice. I'm sure it will be fine."

Another pronounced frown. Clearly, she wasn't adept or remotely interested in hiding her feelings. "Mr. Nicholas told me you should join him in the breakfast room as soon as you are ready."

Another smile, "Okay."

"Ma'am?"

She cleared her throat. "I'll be there presently."

The young girl gave her a bit of a nod and then exited quickly. She had no doubt her Mama, Jessamine, would be getting an earful. And then she became conscious of the fact that she also had no idea what time it was or any remote idea of where the breakfast room was. Well, how big could the place be? So, she quickly checked her appearance in the huge round mirror atop the dresser. Alice had pulled her hair up and twisted it into a curious, poufy hairstyle with a bun on top. She frowned. She had no idea that her hair was capable of such a contortion. Without further contemplation, Julia headed out the door, leaving the peculiar hat perched atop the ceramic pitcher. In the early morning light, she'd come to the conclusion that the sooner she gave Mr. Nicholas Burke what he wanted, the sooner he would return her home and be out of her life.

She headed into the hallway with a swish of her long navy-blue linen skirt. It irritated her. It was warm and uncomfortable, and Julia resented wearing it. She hesitated at the top of the long spiral staircase, taking a deep breath. She reminded herself that she had to play along. That was the way out of this. Her aunt had intimated as much, or so she gleaned. She tried to ban all thoughts of irritation and frustration. Slowly, she wound down the curving staircase. The short black boots that

Alice had laced her up in were solid but unfamiliar. It was summer. She didn't wear closed-in shoes—flip-flops and sandals at best. Good grief, if he had to choose a time frame, why not the sixties when clothing made sense, and people didn't care what anyone else thought?

She reached the landing, pulling her long skirt away from its awkward entanglement in the staircase. She wandered into the parlor, for lack of a better word, that she had been in the night before. Ahead, she was sure was the connecting room and beyond the short hallway that led to the front door. The weight of disappointment settled in her heart. Last night, the road to home seemed so simple, and in the morning light, given her aunt's input, it seemed more of an unreachable dream. Sighing, she remembered there were no other rooms connected in that direction.

She turned a bit, recalling the other room she'd visited last night. Taking a deep breath, she crossed another threshold and then another to a rather large cypress door, which was closed. Alice had said the breakfast room, so he probably wasn't even in his study. On impulse, Julia raised her hand, giving the door a quick knock. She waited — no answer, then glanced around, trying to plot a new course when the heavy door abruptly swung open.

Nicholas Burke stood in the doorway, shirt untucked over his pants and vest also unbuttoned, hung loosely around his shoulders. Evidently, she wasn't the only one who found the wardrobe unnatural. His hair seemed a bit disheveled, and he decidedly looked surprised. "You're up," he said.

"Yes, were you sleeping in there?" she asked impetuously.

He looked slightly jolted at the inquiry, glancing behind him momentarily in disorientation. "Well, yes, I couldn't sleep, so I came in here to read and—"

63

"Fell asleep," she completed the thought flatly.

He frowned, taking in her apparel, it seemed, for the first time. "You're dressed."

"Yes, it's awful, thank you very much. Alice told me to meet you in the breakfast room, but since I have no earthly idea where that might be."

"The house isn't that big, just a Creole cottage," he murmured.

"Be that as it may. Well, where is the breakfast room?"

He seemed to be listening to her but also somewhere else. "You don't look bad. It actually suits you a bit."

"Breakfast room!" she repeated with irritation. He stepped back a bit, running his hand through his hair. "In here first, we need to take care of some things."

Reluctantly, she stepped into the study. It was pretty unchanged from the night before except for some books strewn about the table and a ceramic mug—coffee, tea, or something else. What exactly did madmen drink late at night when their conscience prickled them, not allowing them to sleep? She crossed to the far side of the room, spinning around a bit on the heel of her black lace-up boots. "What did you want?" she asked curtly.

He softly closed the door and reached atop one of the shorter bookshelves for a rather large leather bag that looked curiously like an old-time doctor's bag. From within, he pulled out a smaller black bag with a short zipper around it and then handed it to her. It suddenly dawned on her what he was up to as she unzipped the small blood glucometer. "You should see how you are doing."

She sat down slowly in front of the long library table, pulled the machine out, and then glanced up at him. His eyes were focused intently on her. "Are you going to watch me?" she asked.

He looked at her with a bit of surprise. "Is it something private?"

"Yes, for me." He nodded in acknowledgment and headed across the room to the fireplace.

"I have regular and NPH insulin."

"I take Lantus."

"Well, I'm afraid you'll have to make do for a bit."

"Lovely," she murmured. She jabbed her finger with the lancet, touching the test strip with a drop of blood, and then waited for the few seconds it took to get the result. The screen flashed back, 238—high, but not as high as she'd expected, given that she'd been without insulin for several days.

"How is it?" he asked.

"Where's the insulin?" she replied abruptly, ignoring his inquiry.

He returned to her, stopping in front of the short rectangular table. "You know Julia, for us to be successful, we're going to have to work together. And I need you to be in good health to do so. So again, how is it?"

She swallowed, a little startled by his sudden shift in mood from disheveled to commanding. "A bit high, 238."

He nodded, "Well, could be worse. I'll get the insulin. It's on ice in the kitchen."

"Must have Jessamine curious," she quipped.

"No, she knows I'm a doctor and leaves my medicines alone."

She looked at him with surprise. "You're a doctor?"

He paused at the doorway, "Yes, I have an MD in psychiatry. And as I said, I can give you the injections if you're not comfortable."

She shook her head, "No, I'll handle it myself."

He turned to her again. "You know, it would help if you could trust me just a little, Julia."

"Trust has to be earned," she replied softly. There was a hesitation on his part, and then he left the room without another word.

Mrs. Burke Puts Her Foot Down

Chapter Eleven

The breakfast room painfully reminded her of the sunroom of her parents' house at Solomon Place, not as much in detail as in essence. It was situated to the back of the Creole Cottage, as Nicholas had deemed it, a large airy space with an oval table made of a lighter wood that looked suspiciously like pine and white French doors leading out onto a garden courtyard. The energy flowed in with the morning light, filling her with longing for what was familiar.

Only a few moments earlier, Nicholas had retrieved the two vials of insulin as well as a syringe and alcohol swabs. He didn't wait for her to give herself an injection, just curtly requested that she return everything to the doctor's bag and then meet him in the breakfast room, to which he gave her rather abrupt directions. The whole exchange took a matter of seconds and left her befuddled. Then again, as strained as their last exchange was, she shouldn't be surprised that he didn't want a repeat.

It had literally been years since she'd used a syringe for an injection. But she did as requested, returning everything to the black leather bag. She was certain he would return the vials to the kitchen in due course. One thing that she had gleaned from Nicholas Burke was that he was thorough.

It was only a quick left past the study and passage through a sort of den, which led her into the breakfast room. Oddly enough, it was completely deserted. She sat at the long table, deeply wishing for another time or perhaps a friendly face.

Nicholas entered shortly after her arrival — changed, buttoned up, properly in another suit, looking more like a man of their particular day. He smiled, "Everything all right?"

She looked at him a bit blankly, "In what sense?"

He nodded, "Right, well, Alice will be along with coffee and some biscuits, I think presently."

She narrowed her eyes, "Are you rich?"

"Excuse me?"

"I was wondering if you are rich. How does one maintain a domicile in another time frame?"

He frowned at the inquiry, "It's complicated, and I would prefer that you don't discuss this in front of Alice or her mother."

"Why not? They think I'm crazy anyway."

"Not crazy, Julia, ill."

She sighed, "Fine distinctions. How is it that you and Christian are looking for the same thing?"

He settled in a chair across from her at the table. "How well do you know him?"

"You didn't answer my question."

"We are collectors."

"Collectors? Of what?"

"I suppose you could say esoteric treasures. Now, answer my question."

"How well do I know him? I don't know. How well can you know someone in two days?"

"Two days, is that all?"

She nodded, "Yes, but he seemed sincere."

"Really? And this you gleaned in two days?"

"Well, as far as I know, he hasn't kidnapped anyone."

But before he could respond, Alice appeared in the doorway with a rather large tray of food. Nicholas' face mutated into a wide smile. "Ah, thank you, Alice. As you can see, Mrs. Burke is looking much better this morning." Julia shot him an irritated glance at his use of that title.

The young girl smiled in response to his graciousness. "Yes, Mr. Nicholas, I know you are happy to have your wife home again." Julia stared dismally down at the plate of food that Alice had placed in front of her only seconds before. "Though Mrs. Burke has taken a disliking to her clothing."

She looked up now sharply at the both of them with surprise. Nicholas took a sip from the porcelain coffee cup Alice had also brought. "Is that so?"

"Yes, sir, Mrs. Burke refused to put on all her undergarments."

"Hey," Julia snapped out uncontrollably. "Please don't talk about me when I'm sitting right here."

Alice smiled a little sheepishly, "I'm sorry, Mrs. Burke. I just thought maybe it still had something to do with your illness."

Nicholas leaned back in the wooden chair, eying Julia with an indiscernible expression. "Was it anything terribly essential?" he asked.

Alice opened her mouth to answer when Julia interceded. "I think that's quite enough, Alice. My undergarments are no business of Mr. Burke's."

Alice gave Nicholas a quick glance, and he nodded as if to say he concurred with his pseudo-wife. "Thank you, Alice. I think we can handle things from here."

She nodded, giving Julia a parting glance that told her explicitly that she was not at all pleased with the way things had proceeded. She stared at him pointedly at Alice's exit. "Was that really necessary?"

"She takes her job seriously. You better eat. I have a busy morning planned, and I don't want you collapsing on me."

She expected that they would be going out. In fact, she was wholly prepared for it. But instead, after breakfast and half an hour of freshening up, she was summoned by Alice to another room. It was one she hadn't seen before, but again, in this house, that seemed a rather common occurrence. It appeared to be a small private sitting room of sorts at the end of the long hallway on the second floor. Alice smiled and asked if she needed anything, perhaps a cup of tea. Instead, Julia quietly inquired about the purpose of this peculiar little room. It had an old-fashioned desk and chair against the wall. There was also a short sofa, about loveseat size, and a long chaise lounge chair. "Why, this is where Dr. Burke sees his patients." Alice answered.

"His patients?" she asked the girl. "He actually has patients here?"

And then a mark of confusion crossed her face. "Well, we assume so. We've heard conversations in here, sometimes late at night. He's a very private man, Mr. Nicholas."

And Julia had smiled, understanding that Alice's knowledge was limited in this matter and more so than that what she was willing to share with her in particular was also within limitation. So, Alice had left her there, gloves on, and even that silly hat perched atop her head in anticipation of at least temporarily being sprung. But here she was, trapped in an even smaller room than before. She pulled off the white gloves with disgust, tossing them onto the rose-colored antique loveseat soon to be followed by the ridiculous navy blue hat. Then she plopped herself down onto the long matching chaise, closing her eyes while feeling tears of frustration and depression threatening to eke out. Within a few moments, the door swung open.

She didn't even acknowledge his entry, just waited as she heard the door close behind him. "I thought we were going out," she murmured hotly. The façade of pretending to cooperate was wearing more than thin on her nerves.

"Not yet," he replied softly.

She turned to look at him as he settled into the wooden chair in front of his desk. "You know, it's insane for you to keep me here. I can't help you. I can't take much more of this."

He glanced over to her, his expression dark and unreadable. "I'm sorry it's been difficult for you. That's why I thought we would start this way."

She sat up a bit from her reclining position. "What way?" she asked.

"I want to hypnotize you," he said calmly as if he'd said he wanted to brush his teeth.

She felt completely stunned by his words. "Oh really? Well, that's never going to happen."

He frowned, "From your demeanor, I gather you want to go home."

Damn him, constantly holding this over her head. "God, you're not being fair."

His stare was disturbing, penetrative. "I need to understand what you know, Julia." She suddenly felt her head swirl in dizziness, and she closed her eyes to try to reorient. She heard something as though he were pulling his chair closer to her beside the chaise. "Lie back, try to relax." She shook her head, but she felt his hands on her, pushing her back into the semi-reclining position that the chair afforded.

"I can't tell you anything," she whispered as she felt the pressure of his hand across her forehead. "I can't trust you."

"You can," his voice was soothing. "I'm not going to hurt you. Let me see."

Her eyes opened almost involuntarily, and he was there beside her, staring back at her with that dark intensity and the flood of familiarity. "I know. I feel it, too," he whispered.

"I know you," she answered, compelled not at all because she wanted to.

She felt his hand against her cheek caressing, sending tendrils of sensation along her skin, but she knew it was because he wanted something — all of this only because he wanted something. "Show me," he insisted. And then she closed her eyes and felt herself take flight.

Back to Solomon Place

Chapter Twelve

She opened her eyes to her sunroom at Solomon Place as though she'd simply been lounging on the short wicker sofa against the far wall. She slowly sat up. The early morning light was streaming in through the long picture windows. Glancing over, she could see her art table was still there, untouched, and in its corner, a mug of coffee as though she'd just left it to come over and take a nap. She breathed deeply with relief and then stopped, standing up — comfortable, familiar. "Stop playing games with me, Nicholas," she said sharply.

"I'm not playing games," he responded. He was sitting across the room in one of the white rattan chairs her mother had placed around the sunroom. He looked different to her, more relaxed, more casual in a white polo shirt and khaki pants, not the antiquated clothes she had always seen him in. "I wanted you to feel comfortable so we could talk more easily."

She stared outside into the yard. The short granite birdbath was covered with a flock of sparrows. "This is a torment, being here."

"You don't seem tormented," he commented. "You seem calmer. If there is somewhere else, you would prefer Julia."

"It's not right — you having free access to my mind like this, my memories."

He laughed softly, "You overestimate me. Your mind is filled with barriers, locked doors, twists and turns."

She relaxed ever so slightly. "It's so peaceful here."

"Yes, a refuge," he agreed. "Your parents must have been happy."

"I think so. They seemed content with their lives."

"That's why the house is like this. The energy they left here." She wasn't looking at him, just outside at the play of birds and squirrels only yards away. "When did you first begin seeing your aunt?" he asked.

She turned to him, "My aunt?"

He was still sitting there. His legs stretched out comfortably in front of him as though they were just having a casual morning chat. "Yes, your Great Aunt Lilia. It seems to have made a great impression on you."

She frowned, "Yes, well, wouldn't talking to a spirit make an impression on you?"

"Yes, I suppose it would. When?"

She turned away, crossing her arms. She didn't want to submit to his prodding or answer his questions. She just wanted to stand here and soak up the serenity, but his voice was subtly compelling. "It was after my parents' death, after Peter and I split up."

"Peter?" he prodded.

"Yes, my ex-husband, after my parents' death, our marriage fell apart."

"Because of their death?"

She shook her head, feeling that black time of despair creeping over her again. "No, because I was too tired to try to hold it together anymore."

He was silent, though she could feel him near her mind, feeling considering. "I see. It must have been difficult."

She laughed softly, "You think?" and then continued talking almost to herself. "It takes so much energy to pretend you're not yourself — to pretend you're somebody someone else wants you to be."

"Is that what he wanted?"

"It seemed to be the only way to keep the peace, so draining, so exhausting. And then my parents were gone, and the grief took every ounce of energy I had left. By the time my aunt came to me, I was—"

"In despair," he offered.

"In hopelessness," she said softly.

"I'm sorry," he said.

She turned to him with surprise. "Are you?" she asked. But there was no expression she could read on his face.

"Yes," she could feel his emotions — strange, deep, turbulent, calculating. Apparently, this exchange between them was reciprocal. She could feel an intense pull, a need within him, powerful — so much determination. And then she could feel and see the texture of a cold, drafty stone room, archaic with echoes and voices — tables layered with equipment, but not modern, antiquated. And then his voice, "If you push too much, Julia, you might learn things you're not ready for." She stepped back away from his consciousness. He was looking at her intently, not with upset but with curiosity. "You have a powerful mind."

"Where are you going with all this?" she asked shakily.

"I wanted you to be calm. Now, I want you to show me everything that occurred with Christian from the first moment you met him." She felt a swirl of dizziness again, then quietly sat on the sofa. He had moved over to her, standing in front of her and taking her hand. She'd thought to resist, then realized it was pointless. Besides, at this point, there didn't seem any reason to protect Christian. She knew about as much about him as she did about Dr. Nicholas Burke.

Sleep came broken and clouded — a house long ago and whispers that raged in his mind like distant screams. It was a pressure that seethed in his head from when he was a young boy — a pressure exacerbated by anger. He stood in the shadows down the long gallery at his father's house, his father's house that, for the last two years, had belonged to him. He was the master now of it all, and as he breathed, the pressure raged in his head, and the pain stabbed at his heart. He watched his cousin Antoine and his young bride of just a few months together. The bastard didn't even have the decency to take her indoors. He had her pressed against the walls of his father's house, making love to his wife in the shadows. But he just watched and waited, the pressure building even as the cold anger grew.

It tore through him painfully, her beautiful face exuding such expressions of passion and ecstasy. It was something he'd never seen before with her. She was always so placid and distant, but not now, not with Antoine. It stirred him deeper than anger, than betrayal—this envy, complete and total envy.

Christian sat up in bed. It was light outside. He picked up his watch, just two. Now he remembered. He'd just thought to close his eyes briefly to shake the fatigue that had clung to him for the past several days. But his head still throbbed from the dream. It wasn't unfamiliar. It was one that had repeated with him intermittently during his lifetime. He breathed deeply, trying to clear his mind, clearing away the intense, painful emotions that always seemed to accompany it. He could still see her face in his mind so clearly, and her eyes.

He leaned back onto the pillow for a moment focusing again on the eyes — so familiar. It dug at him. Closing his own eyes, he followed the thread but again came up against the fog, a barrier. With all his energy, he pushed through it until he actually heard a shattering like glass. It was accompanied by pain, blinding sharp pain, but he persevered until the pieces slowly began to come back to him.

He followed them closely. He watched Christian intercepting Julia on St. Ann's street. He knew it was risky. It could break the fugue he had placed in Christian's mind when he'd taken Julia. But he was a pragmatist. It was only a matter of time before that happened anyway. Without him actually being in the same vicinity to reinforce it, the block would naturally weaken and deteriorate. So, he gambled, gambled that there was some information here worth obtaining. And then she'd collapsed unexpectedly.

He moved closer toward her. He could feel it around her, strange, like stepping into an electromagnetic field. All around her, the energy was different, stronger, and more vibrant. He ignored Christian and concentrated only on where her awareness lay. He sunk deeper into her mind. She was seeing it, seeing the prism of energy. It was wrapped around her, connecting for only a few seconds, and then it fled.

In fact, it was when he touched her, Christian, to revive her that it fled. Nicholas stepped back. He hadn't been wrong. She was the key somehow. She was undeniably the key here.

She opened her eyes, and unexplained tears were streaming down her face. She tried to sit up slowly, but she ached. Every part of her, every inch of her ached.

He stood across from her in the room by the door, watching her. And then she'd remembered. He'd walked in early this morning without a word and struck her violently across the face so that she slammed against the headboard of the bed and lost consciousness. She pulled herself up to a sitting position. "Did you really think you could get away with this?" he asked coldly.

Julia opened her eyes with a jolt. Her heart was slamming in her chest. Nicholas was sitting next to her, staring at her with concern. "What is it?" he asked. "What did you see?"

She shook her head, still feeling as though her entire body was trembling. "I don't know. I don't know."

He was beside her, and then he closed his eyes, touching her face with the palm of his hand. It still stung there where she was hit. But then she tried to clear the fog. No, she wasn't really hit. It was just a dream. She moved to pull away from him, but Nicholas said softly, "Be still."

"It doesn't matter. I was just dreaming."

His dark eyes widened, staring at her intently. "Have you had visions of this sort before, this intense?"

She swallowed, debating how much to tell him. He was being so comforting now, but that was only now. "I don't know. I suppose."

He frowned, "Doesn't feel like a dream. It's too intense, too exact."

"Well, what else could it be?" she asked.

But he stared back at her solemnly, not even attempting to answer the question before him.

The Waking Dream

Chapter Thirteen

Nicholas returned to his bedroom. He'd suggested that Julia rest the remainder of the morning, and then after lunch, they go out. He was tired, exhausted, actually feeling quite drained from their exploration earlier. And then how it had unexpectedly ended. He stared out of his window down to the courtyard below. He had told himself he preferred this time frame. It wasn't the first time he'd visited and even toyed with the idea of living his life out here once he'd accomplished what was promised. He'd told himself it was less complicated here, but what had just happened was clearly sending a different message. It seemed that old baggage followed you wherever you traveled.

He knew he was tied to Julia and had glimpses enough to know just how much he was tied to her. But he'd honestly had hoped to keep all of that separate. Like a good scientist, it was essential to keep things distilled and pure. Unfortunately, life didn't work that way. Everything was intimately interconnected. Finding the elemental was opening all sorts of doors, doors that, for all their sakes, might be best served remaining closed.

Julia was tired. Her jaw ached, and she was tired. Her skin throbbed, too, with an awareness. She skimmed her hands along the cool brass footboard of the bed, her fingertips chilling at the contact. But her mind swirled with whispers, *"What are you talking about?"*

"Last night, I saw you with my cousin, you faithless whore."

Her head swirled with the dizziness.

"This is dangerous, my dear."

She focused on the image of her aunt standing across the room. "What is?" she whispered. Her head still ached and swirled with the smells and sensations of somewhere else. She could feel the fear rolling in her stomach, so real, so tangible. "Things are unstable. It would be disastrous for you to slip into that other place."

"Slip into where?" She was trying to focus, trying to concentrate on her aunt, but she was becoming blurry, fluctuating. She felt herself sink onto the bed, her body falling down against its softness. And by the door, she could see the faint image of that man, the other man, so angry, so enraged.

Nicholas had just closed his eyes, finally deciding to rest, when he heard a startling whisper. *"Quickly, it's Julia. Your traveling has made things unstable. She's slipping away."* He jolted up in his bed and, without a thought, headed down the hall.

"Julia, focus, focus on my voice," her aunt's directions, but distantly. And the man, the angry man across the room, was becoming clearer. She'd tried to answer him, but she couldn't. The pain was too great.

And then she felt hands on her, shaking her — energy pouring from his hands. "Julia, Julia, come back."

"I'm so sorry," she whispered. "I can't help it. I love him. Just let me go."

The hands gripped her painfully, but she couldn't see anything but a swirl, and red, a red glow bleeding everywhere. She could feel the hands touching her, pulling the neckline of her dress roughly down and touching her skin, her heart area, pouring energy into her. "Focus, fight to be here, Julia," he rasped.

And then he was pulling her against him, kissing her just like the night before. Her mind swirled, and her arms went around him instinctively. He would save her. He would. And then she stopped. She turned her head and saw clearly the bedroom — the bedroom, the Creole cottage. He was still kissing her, holding her, kissing her skin — her neck. And everywhere he touched, every part of her was responding to him wildly.

But then, the cold realization hit her mind fiercely, if not the rest of her. She yanked herself from his embrace, springing frantically to her feet beside the bed. "What are you doing?"

He stared at her, eyes glazed, as though trying to assimilate exactly what she was asking. And then the fog seemed to clear, and he did the unthinkable. He started laughing softly. "Trying to stop you from slipping away."

She was breathing deeply, trying to pull the neckline of her dress back up into a seemlier position. Her eyes flew around the room. She remembered the man standing by the door, how he'd hit her, but it was a different place. Nicholas sat up on the bed, putting his legs over the side, then softly grabbed her hands, pulling her attention back to him. "Where were you, Julia?" She focused on him now, remembering the feel of his hands on her, his lips. "It's all right. You need to tell me."

"I don't know," she felt as though the ground was dropping out beneath her. She was so overcome by emotion. Nicholas pulled her down to sit beside him on the bed and then put his arm around her shoulder, pulling her closer. She felt as though she was trembling all over — first from the trauma of it all and now compounded by his close proximity. But she felt powerless to pull away, powerless to do anything.

"It's all right," he whispered, rubbing her arm with his hand.

"There was a man," she said. "Somewhere else, I know he wanted to kill me."

"You tapped into something."

She felt tears, tears of total devastation falling down her cheeks, but whose devastation? "It was so real," she whispered. "I can still feel the pain where he hit me."

He pulled her closer against his side. "You need to disconnect from this. Right now, it can only be damaging."

"I don't understand. Disconnect from what?" Her breaths were coming deep, and she was panicking.

"Shhh," he continued to rub her arm and hold her against him. She could feel his warmth just flooding into her, calming her. But it didn't make sense. He'd kidnapped her, brought her here against her will. She couldn't be so comforted. "Stop thinking," he said a little forcefully but still in a soothing tone. "Just stop thinking and be."

She closed her eyes and felt herself being lulled into the calmness he offered. There would be no answers now, no understanding, just rest and peace. He scooped his arms under her legs and pulled her fluidly beside him on the bed, enfolding her against him. It was so quick and felt so natural she didn't have a second to protest. "Nicholas," she began.

But he placed his fingertips lightly across her lips. "Not now, Julia. You need to rest. There will be time for everything else later." Her sleepiness spread. She relaxed in his arms since it was clear to her that he wasn't going anywhere.

It was cold but filled with light — the stone floors pale, reflective of light that cascaded to the ivory walls. Even the tables were constructed of hard stone surfaces. Marble? Couldn't be, but she wondered. They were heavy and had the texture.

"You see, it was my fault." The voice floated in but then crashed heavy against the acoustics of the long, bright room. "I tampered with things, with energy, with nature. I shouldn't have tried to bind her into our world."

She heard the voice soft yet sharp and bombastic. It didn't need volume to impact in this room.

"Can you understand that?"

It was closer, the voice, but no body attached to it yet. Was she expected to answer?

"Yes, I would be obliged."

And then she turned to her side and peered into the most crystal-clear eyes, pure blue like the sky, unadulterated blue. It was a man, an older man, maybe in his late sixties or early seventies, with white hair and long robes, long light bluish robes not so different from the color of his eyes. She was dumbstruck. What could she say?

"Do you see now?" He spoke calmly, but again, it felt as though the voice was everywhere. "She suffers here, bound like this."

"Bound?" she questioned.

"I had to protect her, as I couldn't return her to where she came from."

"What do you want from me?" she asked.

Then he reached out and softly touched her forehead, but it burned like fire, fire straight into her mind.

Julia sat straight up in the bed, but it wasn't her bed. And it wasn't the brass bed from Nicholas Burke's Creole cottage. It was somewhere else, a heavy mahogany four-poster bed covered in white sheets and a white bedspread with loose pieces of gauze draping off the sides of the light canopy above her. Her heart clutched violently in fear. She pulled the bedspread tightly up to her chin. And she shut her eyes, praying frantically. It couldn't be. How could it be — that place, that bedroom, that man? She sunk deeply within her mind, then simply screamed.

She opened her eyes again, breathing frantically. But this time, it was the brass bed, and Nicholas sat beside her, hands on her arms, shaking her. "Are you all right?" he asked, a bit out of breath himself. "You seemed to be having a bad dream and then started screaming."

She was trembling, trembling frantically, and then the dizziness and the spots before her eyes. "I need something," she said. "Low blood sugar."

His dark eyes were unguarded, raw with concern. In seconds, he was out of the room. She slumped back onto the pillow. Her heart was still beating so strongly that she was astonished it didn't come right out of her chest.

Entering a More Savage Place

Chapter Fourteen

He watched her closely. She appeared to have stabilized from the hypoglycemic episode thanks to some juice and toast that Alice had prepared. But there was a greater problem at hand that Nicholas was beginning to recognize. He couldn't keep her here much longer.

He stared out the window of her room but didn't see what was before him. His mind was busy analyzing, calculating. For some not wholly unfathomable reason, Julia's transition to this time frame was incomplete and unstable, as her aunt had indicated. He suspected it had to do with her profound empathetic nature. Her psyche was open to so many vibrations that other energy currents, powerful currents were drawing her.

"I'm so tired," she said softly. She was sitting in the bed, having finished eating a few moments before.

"You should rest," he said.

She glanced over at him. Her face was drawn, pale. This, all of this, had taken such a toll on her. Again, he felt a wave of guilt. After all, it was he who was subjecting her to all of this. "I'm afraid to." He sat on the side of the bed next to her. Her eyes were so wide, so unguarded now. Not as they had been when he first brought her here. It was clear to him that whether she wanted to or not, she was beginning to trust him. And he wondered exactly what he'd done lately to earn that.

He lightly touched her cheek with the palm of his hand. "It's all right. I'll stay with you."

And then she looked at him questioningly, "Will that help?"

"I hope so," was the only honest answer he could give.

"So, this bastard just snatched her right from under my nose!"

"It seems so," Gregory responded. They were sitting in a garden beside a monastery in Italy. It was a comfortable spot on a hillside — one he'd had flashes of often in past life regression. It wasn't so surprising that his former friend, now spirit guide, would choose this particular location as a setting to counsel him.

"Where has he taken her?"

The monk shook his head in negation, "It's clouded. Clearly, that was his intent." Christian felt exasperated and, more than that, outraged. How dare he, how dare he have the audacity to interfere. Gregory turned to him, eying him benevolently. "This isn't the place for such violent feelings, my friend. Letting your ego dictate your actions is perilous."

Christian nodded, now attempting to clear his mind of such unevolved emotions. He'd learned long ago that thought produces energy, and all energy has a particular vibration and attraction. So, if one operates through low-level vibrations— anger, envy, greed—it will attract energies at that same level. "Can you tell me at least why he is so intent on obtaining the crystal?"

His friend sighed, "It's difficult. Everything seems to be tied up in karmic obligations."

Again, doors closed. Everywhere he looked, doors closed. "How do I get her back?"

"Are you sure that is the best course, my friend?" Gregory asked.

"Best course?" He was a bit astonished at the question. "You can't think she's better off in that maniac's hands."

He laughed softly, "So, you think she'd be better off in your hands."

"It's my responsibility. I brought her into this."

"I see," Gregory murmured. "Everything that's happening has to do with bonds—energy bonds, bonds created long ago. I suppose the most effective avenue to destabilize Nicholas Burke's actions would be to focus on the bonds you share with her."

"Bonds?" he asked. Then a flurry of images cascaded across his mind of another time, another life. "I understand," he murmured.

"But I caution you, my friend. Consider carefully before you make a choice, because once selected, you will be obliged to accept all its consequences."

He watched her sleep — calmly, serenely, and exerting great effort to ensure she stayed exactly where she was, in her body, in this room.

"How long do you think you can keep this up?"

Nicholas' eyes followed the voice, the same voice that had warned him earlier of Julia's danger. He could hear it, but at the moment, he could not connect it to a form. "As long as I have to," he replied.

While focusing on the protective barriers he had placed around Julia, he allowed his mind to open a bit and be receptive. A form began to solidify in the corner of the room, from transparency and shifting colors to more solid, recognizable — a woman in a long dark dress. "You're the aunt."

"Yes, you're gambling quite a bit with my great-niece."

His eyes returned to the sleeping figure on the bed, "I need her."

"In what sense?" she asked coolly.

He turned back to her. "It's essential—"

"That you find the elemental." She completed his thought. "So, I've heard."

He frowned. It was clear the great aunt was here to give him a hard time, just what he needed at the moment. "It suffers."

She nodded, "Yes, suffering for which you are responsible. Tell me, Mr. Burke. How exactly do you expect to alleviate its suffering by inflicting suffering on Julia?"

"That is not my intention."

"Yes, well, we all know what the road to hell is paved with."

Her face was passive as she delivered such biting observations. "You certainly are a caustic woman, Aunt Lilia."

"I don't believe in varnishing the truth."

He laughed softly, "Well, I might yet surprise you and save everyone."

"Does that include yourself, Mr. Burke?" she asked quietly. But he didn't answer, and it didn't matter because he was already alone with Julia again.

The ends justify the means. Perhaps, that was the justification he was using. Once Julia was back, safe from wherever Dr. Nicholas Burke had whisked her off, then he could set things right. He focused deeply, satisfied with justifying his actions. Of course, he knew of his connection to her. Not initially, perhaps when they'd first met, but after some limited exposure, it became clear to him where they had crossed paths before.

For the past three days, he had conducted a meditation, a focused one. The image that was clearest to him was the house, a tremendous sprawling antebellum home not far from the banks of the Mississippi River. Strangely for him, the bond felt stronger to the house than any particular person within, connected by history, connected by blood and pride. And as he allowed his consciousness to enter this world again, his higher faculties dimmed, and his mind entered a more savage place — something that Gregory would term a predatory setting. As he'd once said, *"We're so convinced we're more evolved than animals, but we do more evil to feed our egos than they could ever contemplate."*

So, Christian had been focusing on that time, that place, and the woman Julia had been.

He could have allowed judgment or his moral compass to interfere, but that would have prevented his goal. Instead, he allowed his mind to embrace the understanding that these were different times. After all, in the Dark Ages and for some time after, people held themselves to a different standard of conduct. Higher thinking was suspended in favor of more primal considerations. He tried not to judge the actions of Philippe Charbonnet, the man he had formerly been but rather used him as a vehicle to get what he wanted.

As he breathed deeply and focused his concentration on this other time, this other place, he felt himself sink into the mind of his former self. It was a mind that was limited, pragmatic, and fearful, which one might find extraordinary for the owner of a profitable sugar plantation in the pre-civil war era. Of course, certainly, there was always the stress of living up to the expectations of everyone around him. Some might consider him a tragic figure, but most perhaps not.

And so, determined to reach deeper, Christian obliged himself to relinquish his control for the moment, his thinking, and sink yet further.

He could feel the body, afflicted in some way — aches and pains running along his arms and beneath his knees, something unspoken, undiagnosed. And he watched her from a window outside, talking to some locals passing through. She smiled, she laughed. She seemed so young and carefree — Ovelia. He envied her nature, her liveliness, and it angered him. He couldn't ever remember a time of being without care. Responsibility was thrust upon him at so young an age. But the consciousness of Christian focused on her, focused on drawing her here. She stopped her conversation and turned back toward the house. Their eyes met, but everything about her had changed. All the life and joy had drained out of her and been replaced with what he could only identify as fear. Strong emotion was the key. Together, Christian and Philippe Charbonnet smiled at their success.

An Evening Appointment

Chapter Fifteen

Her eyes flickered open gradually. The room was still filled with light, although not as brightly as before. She could see it seeping through the slightly parted drapes beside the bed. Slowly, she focused on the figure sitting in the chair just next to the door. It was Alice, actually Alice looking a little bored. Clearing her throat, "Alice," she managed in a heavy whisper. She'd been sleeping so heavily that she questioned whether her vocal cords were functioning. The young girl, who moments before had seemed to be focused on everything except her, now zoomed in directly on her face in surprise.

"Miss Julia," she said.

She wondered a little abstractly when she had become Miss Julia instead of Mrs. Burke. "What are you doing here?" She did sound croaky, more than a bit on the raspy side.

"Watching you," she answered, as if it was ridiculously obvious. And then she began to elaborate, which Julia had known would happen if she waited long enough. "You've been sleeping nearly all day. We were afraid you were becoming sick all over again. Do you know what time it is? It's nearly six."

Julia tried to sit up in the bed but felt her head swirl a bit. Damn, the blood sugar. If she'd been asleep that long, how many meals had she skipped? Alice was already on her feet. "I have to get Mr. Nicholas. He insisted I get him if anything at all happened."

"Anything?" she repeated.

Alice nodded, "I'll be back." And she disappeared through the door. Julia swung her feet over to the side of the bed, trying to shake off the very heavy sleep she'd just emerged from. There had been no more dreams, at least none she could pull to mind — only rest, heavy, coma-like rest. She glanced up, feeling the sudden shift in energy around her. Nicholas was standing at the door, watching her gravely.

"How do you feel?" he asked.

Her head spun a bit at the question, literally and figuratively. "Dizzy," she replied. He moved to sit beside her on the bed, lightly placing his hand on her forehead as if to check her temperature. "You're a bit warm," he murmured. "But that could be from the sleep."

"I was wondering," she said quietly, "how I could possibly help you find this crystal if I'm always sick or asleep."

"You will," he said. "You should check your blood sugar, then I'll have Alice get you something to eat. He stood up next to her. "We have an appointment this evening."

"What kind of appointment?" she asked a bit suspiciously.

"We'll talk about it when you feel better. Would you like to take a carriage ride this evening?"

The thought of being outside the house brought a brush of hopefulness and anticipation she'd lacked since this whole thing began.

"Yes," she responded. "I would like that."

And a slight smile of validation crossed his lips at her reply.

Momentarily, it seemed to have subsided. Whatever intense energy was pulling her so strongly to another time frame had eased. But he wasn't complacent. He imagined it functioned not so unlike the tides, strong and powerful at moments and ebbing at others. So, Nicholas watched vigilantly.

Her blood sugar was running low, but given how little she'd eaten during the day, that wasn't very surprising. After her evening dose of insulin, he insisted Alice bring her a rather substantial tray of food, which he watched her eat. Every now and then, Julia would meet him with a quizzical expression as if to say, "Don't you have anything better to do?"

But he ignored it. At the moment, she was more like a patient under his care, and it was his responsibility to make sure that nothing happened to her. But he waited until Alice cleared the tray before broaching a delicate subject. "Feeling better?" he asked.

She looked at him again with an odd, questioning expression. He hadn't had time to think of it much, given the urgency and chaos of the day. But things had changed between them considerably and quickly. Hours ago, he'd held her intimately in his arms, kissing her, and then not long later held her again until she slept. Her eyes reflected a slight confusion, keying him into the fact that she was in tune with his thoughts. "Yes, less shaky," she replied, not returning his gaze.

He considered carefully. Was it time to clear the air or time to leave the pink elephant in the room to its own devices? "I'm going to send Alice in to help you change," he stated rather casually.

She frowned, "Why am I changing?"

He'd opted to leave the elephant alone for the moment. After all, there were other fish to fry. "I told you we have an appointment," he replied smoothly.

Now she looked at him directly, unflinchingly. "Yes, I remember now. An appointment I have to change for?"

"This is 1910."

"Your point?"

"People dress in the evening for events."

She raised an eyebrow, "Are we going to the opera?"

He shook his head, "No, it's not exactly entertainment. Though I suppose some may view it as such."

"I'm not enjoying your crypticness, Mr. Burke."

He rested his hands on the brass footboard of her bed. So, it was back to Mr. Burke after all. But then he stopped himself. Ah, yes, they were presently ignoring the elephant. "I don't mean to be cryptic, Julia." He allowed his voice to linger on her name perhaps a bit too long.

She straightened up her back a bit. She didn't really like not being in control, not at all, he suspected. "Where are we going?" she asked directly.

"To visit an acquaintance of mine — Josephine Delachaise."

She eyed him strangely, "Pourquoi?"

He smiled at her use of the French interrogative, "Well, Mademoiselle, we are visiting Madame Delachaise to attend a séance."

All vestiges of humor dropped off her face, and he was more than sorry to see them go. "A séance?"

"Yes, I actually think you'll enjoy it. People of this day had more of a flair for the dramatic. Not all that stark, modern Blair Witch kind of attitude."

"What possible purpose do you think a séance will serve?" she said with great exasperation.

"Energy," he said flatly.

"What does that mean? Energy?"

"These events are always sparked by a tremendous flux of energy. It might help spark something with you."

"And if it doesn't?"

"If it doesn't, then we'll have enjoyed an entertaining evening."

She looked at him, frowning, "When you brought me here, Nicholas, did you have any sort of plan?"

He smiled at her pointed jab. "I'll send Alice in," he said, heading to the door. "And Julia," he added before exiting. "Do try to relax a bit."

Embracing the Façade

Chapter Sixteen

The gown was lovely, though it made her feel like she was dressing up for carnival. She examined her reflection in the long mirror in the corner of the room. The waist was high, marked conspicuously by a large piece of satin around it, and the long skirt underneath was the palest of blue colors. It felt like silk, but she wasn't sure. The entire gown was draped by a soft chiffon sort of outer layer — a delicate but intricate garment.

And it made Julia feel strange, altered in some way. She had worn full-length, elaborate dresses before. In fact, she'd worn a wedding dress, although it was tea length, more practical. But she couldn't ever remember in her whole life putting on something that was quite so feminine. And the shocking thing was that it seemed to suit her features. She did not feel as clumsily out of place in it as she might have anticipated.

She smiled at her reflection. Yes, at least outwardly, she could pass for some cultured Edwardian lady. Alice had expertly twisted her long hair up in a soft style and decorated it with a few gardenias that she'd taken from the garden. For the first time, she softly asked herself what life would be like here if she never went home. If she could be the woman, she saw in the reflection before her. And then she thought about Nicholas Burke and felt her heart react unexpectedly, as though it had stilled at the thought of him, of his gentleness, of his ferocity. Again, she eyed the woman in the reflection. Was she completely mad to be entertaining such thoughts? This wasn't a fairy tale.

And then, as if to answer her deep concerns, the door swept open abruptly as Nicholas sauntered into the room and then stopped right in front of her. He was dressed up, too, in a tuxedo, given a tuxedo of the day, but also oddly transformed. "Don't you knock?" she replied flatly.

"Alice said you were ready." And then he smiled broadly, "How wonderful you look, Julia. I thought the color might suit you."

She glanced back at her reflection, feeling disoriented, almost as if she might actually blush. She had to remind herself that this wasn't a prom date. This man had kidnapped her against her will. And then his hands were on her shoulders, softly turning her around to face him. He gently grasped her chin, looking at her intently. "Are you feeling all right? Are you well enough to go out?"

"I didn't realize there was choice involved," she murmured.

He dropped his hand and lightly took her hands in his. He was so tender and pleasant. Did he feel now that somehow their status had shifted? "Tonight, I believe, is important. But I would ask a favor of you."

"A favor?" she repeated somewhat incredulously.

The smile faded a bit. "I can understand why you would think this request is a bit outrageous given the circumstances."

"No more outrageous than anything else you have done."

"Be that as it may, I will ask anyway. I would ask that this evening you try to put everything aside. Forget how you got here, forget—"

"Who I really am?" she filled in impulsively.

And then he softly and completely unexpectedly touched her cheek with his fingertips. "No, that is not what I want. I would like you to relax and enjoy yourself."

"At a séance?"

He smiled, "What you don't realize is that a séance at Josephine Delachaise's house is more like a tea party. It's quite an event."

She couldn't help but smile. After all, what would be the harm if she tried to have a good time?

Once she stepped out of the house, Julia immediately recognized where she was. Mentally, she'd accepted that she'd traveled to 1910. But actually, seeing it in front of her eyes was staggering. It was Royal Street, Royal Street just past Esplanade into the Faubourg Marigny area. She stood on the pavement, frozen, trying to soak in somehow all that was around her. People were strolling on the streets dressed in the attire of the day — women in long tailored dresses, men in antiquated suits, horse-drawn carriages, and children playing but all looking costumed in the period. "It's all right," she heard Nicholas say. He'd walked up just behind her.

"I can't believe this," she murmured mostly to herself.

"That's ours," he indicated.

She glanced up at a black open carriage parked near the house. Her eyes had been so filled by the extraordinary scene that she hadn't even noticed it. Nicholas took her arm and guided her up into the seat. She settled in, pulling the light ivory shawl she wore around her. She continued to stare wide-eyed everywhere as though she were a kid for the first time at an amusement park. He settled in beside her, patting her leg. "Take it easy."

She looked at him with amazement. "I don't know if I really believed it."

He smiled, "And now you do. Take us for a drive along the river and then on to St. Charles," he directed to the driver. She looked at him with a bit of surprise.

"Is that where she lives, on St. Charles Avenue?"

He answered, "Of course."

Even in the year 2011, St. Charles Avenue was one of the more famous areas in New Orleans. The remarkable mansions, all uniquely designed and most remarkably opulent, lined the long stretch from Lee Circle to the River bend where St. Charles intersects with Carrollton Avenue. Julia had admired the grandiose homes from the outside ever since she was a little girl and had toured some of them with her mother as a young woman. But she had never known anyone who lived there. They ran in different social circles than she, and the fact that Dr. Nicholas Burke was taking her now in the year 1910 to a séance there seemed unimaginable. In fact, it seemed like some sort of an illusion.

"How do you know her?" she questioned.

"I've been here before. I've made some acquaintances."

"You've spent enough time—" she stopped herself, glancing up at the well-dressed driver in front of them in the open carriage. She wondered how he would react if she mentioned that his current customers were from the future. "in this place to make such acquaintances?"

He smiled at her. Ever since they'd stepped out of his Creole cottage on Royal Street, he'd adopted a bit of a façade, a nonchalance that Julia assumed had to do with their particular surroundings. Perhaps she should also adopt a world-weary apathy that was more appropriate to the time frame. "Yes, some, relax, my dear. Enjoy your surroundings."

The carriage was rolling very casually down the Avenue at a slow pace. And that essentially was a marked feature of 1910. It was slower here. The pace was easier — not so rushed, not so frantic. There were several other carriages on the road and people strolling, families out for an evening walk, but in better attire than perhaps several blocks before. She sighed deeply. She was a middle-class girl. She certainly didn't feel comfortable rubbing elbows with the very rich.

"I sent a note to Josephine explaining that you've been up North in a hospital recovering from consumption."

She straightened up, more than a bit surprised. "Consumption? Did people recover from that?"

He glanced briefly up to the driver, who hadn't spoken much or changed what she could see of his demeanor since they'd begun their jaunt. "Of course they do, my dear. But I also explained how your prolonged illness might affect your behavior."

She frowned, feeling more nervous now, given the façade Nicholas had created for her. "How very kind of you to make excuses for me before I've even done anything. How did you meet Josephine?"

"She was a patient of mine. She had prolonged bouts of insomnia after her husband died."

"You have patients? Here?" she emphasized.

"A select few," he murmured.

She swallowed, "I thought, well, I assumed you lived closer to my place."

He patted her hand, "I do." Then he pointed forward as the carriage veered off the main road, continuing toward the entrance of an opulent Italianate mansion. She'd seen it many times from her car as she drove down St. Charles Avenue, but never, never, in her wildest dreams had she thought she would set foot in it.

Josephine Delachaise had a butler. Or so Julia assumed, a man dressed like a butler, granted a very old-fashioned butler who answered the door. They were ushered into the foyer of the majestic house, which immediately led to a dazzling massive parlor with a twisting staircase showcased by interior columns as its central features. She stood there, eyes following the room's opulence that culminated in a massive effigy embossed on the ceiling. She felt Nicholas' hand at her back encouraging her forward, but she felt rooted to the spot. It all rushed back to her, those feelings when she had toured the great houses along St. Charles Avenue with her mother — the feelings that crept out and wrapped around her from the very walls. These were old historic places crammed full of energies and, yes, ghosts.

"Are you all right?" he whispered to her.

"Overwhelmed," she whispered back.

Lightly, he placed his hands on her shoulders, and she felt a quick flux of energy from him. "Try to clear your mind and calm yourself."

As if on cue, the butler reappeared from another room that moments before he had disappeared into. "Madame Delachaise and her guests will receive you now."

And then the man turned about fluidly and started leading them in the direction from which he had emerged. Nicholas hooked his arm in hers and quite smoothly escorted her into the lion's den.

Josephine Delachaise's Seance

Chapter Seventeen

Josephine Delachaise was a middle-aged woman. At least, that was what Julia gleaned beneath her expensive, deep purple evening gown and scarves. In addition to the long tapestry shawl she wore loosely draped about her shoulders, she counted at least two other long, exotic-looking scarves — one artfully wrapped in her graying hair and another casually draped around her neck. She supposed it was the 1910 interpretation of a gypsy. But she did smile widely at their entrance, and Julia found that comforting while walking into such an opulent room filled with a small group of opulent-looking people.

"Nicholas," she beamed, embracing both his hands warmly. Julia stood beside him, quietly waiting to be acknowledged, as their hostess warmly hugged and kissed on both cheeks the man posing as her husband. Finally, after what felt like an age, she pulled away from him and turned to Julia. There was an awkward pause for a moment as Julia felt acutely as though she were being surveyed. "And this must be your lovely wife."

"Julia," he offered politely.

"Yes," she spoke in that tone of someone whose mind is distracted. "And how are you feeling, Julia?" she asked softly.

"Well, thank you, happy to be included in your gathering."

Josephine Delachaise smiled gradually and then lightly took Julia's hand, clasping it with both of her own. "I am very happy you can be with us. I know how happy Nicholas must be that you are recovering." Her nearly violet-colored eyes flew to his face briefly and then back to hers. "I'd like to introduce you to my other guests, my dear, before we begin."

Josephine Delachaise was not without her gifts. Nicholas could sense her keen interest in the woman he had labeled as his lovely young wife the moment they were introduced. Josephine could sense much he was sure, but whether or not she could interpret what she was feeling was another matter. Julia radiated a powerful psychic energy, an unusual aura, strong but largely uncontrolled. It was clear Julia's training had been limited, but what was also clear was that she had a tremendous natural talent. All of this combined was something that made her vulnerable as well as formidable at the same time.

For not the first time this evening, he questioned his decision to bring her here. Perhaps, it was a flaw on his part, at odds with his analytical side. It was a compulsion to take risks, risks like bringing Julia to this timeline, risks like trying to escalate her sensibilities here tonight, enabling her to connect with the elemental. Taking risks for oneself was one thing, but dragging another into it was — he glanced across the room. She stood beside Josephine's black marble fireplace, talking to Louis Dugrey and his wife, Marie. He had met them once at a dinner Josephine had hosted some time ago. Strangely enough, Dugrey was a banker, but his wife Marie had a great fondness for Josephine and, oddly enough, the occult. He'd gleaned from Josephine that for the idle rich in this day, exploring the supernatural had become a bit of the rage, not unlike the gadgetry of the cell phone in his day.

As if in response to his intense scrutiny, Julia's eyes turned to his from across the room. They were wide and knowing and then a slight smile crossed her lips before she returned her gaze to Marie Dugrey who seemed intent on captivating her attention. A wave of guilt passed over him, and he wondered what he'd done to deserve that smile except repeatedly risked her well-being.

They'd had tea, although she would have preferred coffee. They had an assortment of sweets, crumbly pastries, and fruity little tart things brought around by servants on trays. She'd lost count of how many servants there were, including the rather stony-faced butler who'd answered the door. And now, they'd adjourned to the oddly shaped table positioned near a rather large bay window. There were just enough chairs, straight-backed, golden tapestry-covered chairs around the rosewood construction, shaped strangely like a cross between an oval and a diamond.

She was seated next to Nicholas, who was next to the Dugreys, with Josephine at what could loosely be called the head of the table, although, to Julia, it seemed more of a point. And on the other side was another widow, Francisca Maxwell, although she wasn't nearly as old as Josephine, perhaps just in her early thirties. And then there was the last couple — the man, Benjamin Lamarque, perhaps in his fifties, with a bit of a flamboyant curling mustache, and his wife, Anne. Julia was positive she was just in her middle twenties. They, amongst all the guests, made her most uncomfortable. Benjamin, she'd observed, undeniably had a roving eye, a roving eye, and a suspicious one, which made her fly to Nicholas' arm. He was a

prosecutor, Josephine explained. And Julia wondered distractedly if trespassing from another time was any kind of criminal
offense, but then Nicholas had been there as if on cue to whisper platitudes and encouragements in her ear. Of course, all in
all, she found it a bit of an odd crew. Although all stylishly and
expensively dressed, she couldn't shake the feeling she was
stuck in some murder mystery dinner. She'd attended one with
Peter once in a restaurant uptown. Then, however, she hadn't
felt like one of the players, and as if some impending doom
were lurking.

A hush seemed to settle in the room, and Julia shifted her
focus from Josephine's guests to the hostess herself. There
were elaborate candelabras lit all over the space surrounding
them. And all the other light fixtures had been extinguished
one by one, almost without her notice. She breathed deeply and
was oddly comforted by Nicholas' presence beside her. The
only other séance she'd ever attended had been at a slumber
party in the sixth grade, a friend's house. But even then, as her
mind was reminded of the long-forgotten memory, she'd found
the whole experience largely uneventful and a tad bit creepy. It
seemed quite natural for her to speak to her Great Aunt Lilia or
to occasionally see those who had passed on. But a séance, the
idea of summoning the dead, felt somehow at odds with her.
After all, if they chose to make their presence apparent, that
was one thing, but this, something compulsory, just hit her a
bit wrong.

"Now, for those new to this, you should take the hand of
those persons on either side of you." Josephine's voice rang out
clear and steady in their now shadowed room. She could see her
face flickering in the candlelight. It was serene, focused. Nicholas had taken her hand, and a bit less forcibly was Anne
Lamarque, who had to reach across the point of the table to

loosely grasp Julia's other hand. A chill passed through her at the contact with Anne. Briefly, she met her dark eyes, but then the young Mrs. Lamarque glanced away. Definitely something amiss here. She felt Nicholas squeeze her hand warmly, and she wondered distractedly how he had been elevated to the stature of her greatest ally in this endeavor — he who had orchestrated everything.

"Now we shall begin," Josephine's voice had elevated somewhat to a higher pitch and become infected with a slight tone of dramatic emotion. Oh well, she supposed that was to be expected given their circumstance. "We call on the forces of the nether world. We come open and willing to receive guidance from the hereafter."

Julia felt a slight chill pass through her at Josephine's proclamation. Her eyes blurred a bit, but then again, she focused on the woman at the head of the table. She could clearly see energy, an intense aura pouring from her body. It was dizzying, ripples of light blue and gold emanating from her. She breathed in deeply. It was more than clear she did have a gift. "Please speak to us from the beyond." Another chill passed through her. And she felt the grip from Anne Lamarque tighten on her hand. Fear passed into her skin from the young woman. She wasn't here by her wish but her husband's. It was too much right now — the flood of panic. But then she could feel Nicholas's strength, grounding strength. It calmed her. "We beseech you. Answer us." There was spinning in her head now, and the room became distorted with the influx of wild energies, uncontained, unfiltered.

It was clear. It was working. There were so many, so many of them vying for a voice, swirling around them all. It was so hot she felt as though she couldn't breathe.

"We feel your presence from the beyond. Alfred, speak to us. I feel you beside me." Josephine's voice had changed, reaching an emotion-filled strident pitch. "Please, my love," she felt the stabbing pain, the anguish in Josephine's voice. She was so desperate to reach him. And there was someone near her, a presence Julia could sense, but it was drowned out in the cacophony of shouting, clamoring — so many who had not accepted the change, who fought to remain part of the flesh. She swallowed painfully. She could feel hands on her, gripping at her in panic. This was no good. There was no order, no protection here. The young woman across from her, Anne, violently wrenched free of her hand and ran out of the room. But her husband aggressively reached across the table and grabbed Julia's hand. She nearly screamed at the contact. In this heightened state, there was no protection. His touch felt like fire pouring into her. She twisted free frantically. "No, no, do not break the connection," Josephine's voice and then she felt the pull from Nicholas. It was just his hand now.

"It's all right, Ovelia. It's all right," she heard his voice and felt his arms around her. But it wasn't him, and she wasn't where she'd been.

A Spiritual Collision

Chapter Eighteen

The darkness wrapped around them, tight like a blanket, muffling thought, hope, and everything but desire. "Ovelia," he whispered in her ear. Stay with me."

Philippe was gone, gone for the week, and his cousin had turned up unexpectedly at the plantation. They'd met before, met at the wedding, a quiet man with dark hair, tall, intense, and mysterious. But they'd had so little contact until he turned up on her doorstep looking for his cousin.

He was cordial, engaging, and, for some odd reason, accessible to her. So, he'd stayed, waiting for Philippe, and every evening, they dined together and, during the days, took long walks near the river. She knew he suspected how unhappy she was, but they didn't talk of it. She thought perhaps she was drawn to him for that reason — at least, that was what her mind told her. But she knew better. No one could understand this. How could they? She didn't. Her upbringing, her character, her thoughts all told her this was wrong. But it didn't matter. And it wasn't because they were weak or sinners. It was because something in their souls, in their God-given spirits, answered to each other. Something that God had arranged outside the sphere of all earthly purpose.

So, when he came to her, to her room in the darkness, she knew this passion would destroy them both. She knew it then and knew it now just as she lay in his arms for the first time. But neither of them could stop it, nor what would come of it.

She stretched out, and her fingers touched the water, which flowed over, through, and about her form like living energy.

As the swirl hit her, like a powerful charge, candescence, it filled her and drowned her. It was too much, too much confusion, too much of everything. And Julia did the only thing she could to stop the onslaught. She opened her mouth and screamed, screamed from the pits of her soul until everything around her crashed into silence.

Nicholas concentrated not on Josephine or her pleas to the other side for contact but wholly on Julia. She was poised to take a journey, and he was bound and determined to accompany her. He opened his vision to connect with hers fully, and he realized she didn't know. The powerful currents sweeping the room were distracting and overwhelming enough for her. It was what he'd hoped for and what he'd feared.

The elemental would be a powerful draw, but as would elsewhere. And it was the latter that initially drew her. He closed his mind and felt her psyche swept to the past, further deeper and more connected than where they were now. He thought about stopping it. Instead, he followed. There was a puzzle here, and all the things were connected like a web. But unfortunately, and not unpredictably, he felt himself drawn and caught in that same web.

Flesh, senses, the humid wrap of the evening — he felt himself settling in a small table on the gallery just for the two of them. He was drinking wine, a dark red, rich wine that was going to his head — making the impossible plausible. She laughed and drew her lacey ivory shawl more tightly around her, but even in the dim light, her face glowed, dazzling. And not for the first time that evening, he contemplated seducing his cousin's wife.

It was painful because the bastard didn't deserve her. All this youth, all this exuberance, and then the way she drew him, tugged at him, completely unconsciously. That was the hell of it. She wasn't a temptress. She just was, was what he needed.

She sipped her glass of wine and smiled. "Would you like more?" she asked him.

He shook his head. He wondered how, how she would receive him. She had offered kindness and friendship with an unguarded nature. And he'd accepted it, being somewhat starved in his life for such simple gifts. And then she'd spoken to him with understanding as though she had free access to all those places that others found so difficult to enter. It was madness, so unexpected. And he considered leaving tonight, not telling her, just disappearing in the darkness. It was the right thing to do. But he felt too weak now to do it as if it was already determined somewhere, a determination that he had no strength to resist.

Her scream shattered the air and broke, well, everything. Julia was still grasping his hand in a frenzied, insane grip. And across from them, Josephine stared at them in total horror, her face blanched to ashen white. He didn't look around. He could only imagine the reactions of the rest of the party but instead scooped a now unconscious Julia up in his arms, carrying her over to a short recamier sofa against the wall. Her skin, her cheek, felt cold to him as he brushed them with his hand. He waited with a nearly panicked concern as her eyes finally began to flicker open. They were cloudy at first, then cleared slowly. "Julia, are you all right?"

But she stared at him in a way that touched recognition, just like the girl from so long ago.

When Julia returned to consciousness, her first thought after clearing the swirling, manic impressions from her mind was how completely embarrassing this whole situation was.

"Do we need to call a physician?" Francisca Maxwell was blurting out.

"I thought her husband was a physician." That must be the deep voice of Louis Dugrey, although just at the moment, she couldn't see his face as Nicholas, Josephine, and Francisca were all bending over her, making her feel more than a tad claustrophobic. Nicholas had her hand clenched in his, truly playing up the role of the panicked husband, although there did seem to be genuine concern in her eyes.

"Her husband is a psychiatrist," Josephine remarked, peering at her from behind Nicholas and Francisca. Then she spoke directly to her. "Are you quite all right, Mrs. Burke?"

Julia squinted her eyes shut for a moment, trying to clear her somewhat blurry vision, then reopened them. They were all there staring at her as if she were some bizarre bug. "I think so," she mumbled, trying to straighten up from her prostrate position on the remarkably uncomfortable little sofa. But the crowd towering over her was making it a bit difficult.

She glanced up at Nicholas, who seemed caught up in his own concerns, for a bit of help. Recognizing her intent, he quite adroitly placed his hand on her back, helping to prop her up and clear the area as the two women stepped back. "Are you sure you are all right?" Josephine questioned again, straightening up but not for an instant, removing the expression of curiosity that marred her features.

As she steadied her feet on Josephine's well-polished mosaic floor, she tried to rally some of her dignity, smiling. "Yes, I think so. Sorry to make such a fuss."

Josephine's curiosity had suddenly mutated into suspicion. "Why did you scream?"

Julia's eyes widened at the pronouncement. Scream? Had she screamed? She turned to Nicholas briefly, and he slightly nodded as if to confirm what Josephine had said. "Well," she said haltingly, "I suppose I was frightened. All of this was, um, kind of spooky."

Josephine eyed her with less than satisfaction, "Are you quite sure you didn't have an experience, Mrs. Burke?"

"An experience?" she asked clueless, though knowing full well where their hostess was headed with this.

"Yes, my dear, a supernatural experience."

She glanced at Nicholas, but his face lacked expression or any indication of how she should respond. "Um, don't think so. It was drafty, though. Didn't you think so?"

Josephine lingered skeptically on her face for a moment, then turned her gaze to Nicholas. "You know, Dr. Burke. You might need to take her home. I don't think she is quite well yet." And then she smiled, becoming hostess again, and quite expertly ushered the rest of the guests into another room for cocktails. Nicholas sat beside her on the sofa, picking up her wrist as if he were feeling her pulse.

"Are you all right?" he murmured under his breath.

It suddenly dawned on her that the party that left the room was a little less populated than it had been at the onset. "Where are the Lamarques?"

He looked up at her a little blankly. "They left. I think you scared them."

She frowned, "I did not."

"Of course you did. You screamed bloody murder — scared everyone in the room."

She hesitated, "Really?"

He nodded, standing up, "We better go. They think you're odd enough."

He held out his hand for her and quite smoothly pulled her to her feet. But he stood there, hesitating for just a moment, staring at her as though something enormous was tangling his thoughts. "What is it?" she asked.

"Later," he responded without elaboration.

The Past Intrudes

Chapter Nineteen

The ride back was largely silent, both Nicholas and the driver, although she hadn't really anticipated any conversation out of the driver. It was largely in darkness except for the illuminated streetlamps and occasional lights near the mansions. She leaned back in the carriage. Funny, she'd never taken the time to think about things like when people started using electricity or cars instead of lovely buggies like the one they were traveling in. She tried to envision what it was like back home now, her little house at Solomon Place. Good thing she didn't have a pet or even goldfish. Who would be there to take care of it, and when would she be going home again?

Nicholas barely spoke at all. She wondered if he was angry with her for her awkward display at Josephine Delachaise's séance. But she didn't feel that. She felt he was caught somewhere deep in his thoughts, considering, analyzing, and rethinking perhaps everything. He helped her out of the carriage when they arrived at his cottage on Royal Street. She waited as he paid the driver — flat rate, she mused, definitely no meter on that thing. And then he escorted her into the house. As she instinctively began to head toward the stairs, he unexpectedly took her arm. "Let's have a drink," he said, in a tone that was simultaneously inviting and yet not a request.

She followed him with curiosity toward his study.

"Brandy?" he asked.

"Yes," she answered. There was awkwardness, tenseness, and the majority of it flowing from him. Something had happened, something odd she didn't understand. She glanced longingly at the unlit fireplace. There was something intrinsically calming about a roaring fireplace. He handed her a brandy glass about a third full, and she considered asking for a bit more but instead said nothing.

"I'm sorry."

He looked at her with a bit of confusion, "Sorry? For what?"

She shrugged, "I get the feeling this didn't go as you hoped."

He sat beside her on the dark brown Chesterfield sofa, which was positioned against a wall of the room. "I honestly didn't know how it would go," he said.

She swallowed a bit nervously, "You didn't?"

He looked at her strangely again, as though he were seeing something he had not seen before. "No, I had no idea what would happen."

"Really, no idea? That sounds a bit dangerous."

He sipped the brandy in a methodical way that made her feel a bit uneasy. "It seemed warranted."

She waited for further explanation, but none seemed to be forthcoming. "What's wrong with you?"

He lowered his glass. "What do you mean?"

"You're acting very strange. Stranger than usual ever since that silly séance."

He smiled a bit, "You think it was silly?"

"Don't you? Josephine and all her odd friends. And what was with that Benjamin Lamarque and his wife?"

He shrugged, "He's essentially a criminal, what you might call a white-collar criminal."

Her eyes widened, "Oh, how lovely. Nice people your friend runs with."

"The world is not so black and white. Most people live in the grays."

"Well, this guy, I think he's definitely running into the dark gray side," she rambled nervously. She didn't understand why he was making her so nervous tonight, even more so than when he first brought her here.

"Why are you so agitated? What did you see?" he asked calmly.

She caught her breath. She knew it would come around to this eventually, but so quickly, so directly. "It was jumbled. It was—"

He stopped her by taking her hand in his. She hated how comforting his touch had become to her. It didn't make sense. It shouldn't be this way. "I don't think that's entirely true, Julia."

She just sat there, feeling like it had become difficult to breathe. "The things I'm seeing, Nicholas, have nothing to do with what you're looking for."

"How can you be so sure?" She thought to answer but couldn't. She didn't know. She didn't understand at all what was happening. "Earlier today, when you became ill. You were having visions of a man, a violent man. You said he wanted to kill you."

"I don't remember that," she murmured. It was all so disjointed, in a swirl.

"Do you remember another time, being another person?"

She could see it easily, the great house, the long gowns, not like the one she wore — different, even more elaborate. "I can see flashes of it," she responded.

"And at the séance?"

She tried reconstructing it in her mind, but it didn't make much sense. "It was so mixed up, so much emotion. Then there was energy, energy, and water flowing over me from somewhere."

"Yes, I had a sense of that as well. Two floods of images, flowing closely, intertwined."

"I don't understand what it means."

"One belongs to a past life that we shared, another to the elemental."

His words had an impact almost like hitting a brick wall. "That we shared?" she repeated hesitantly. And then her heart picked up its beat, a wild beat of fear. She stood up, facing him with more than a bit of panic and accusation. "You're not saying that man I saw—the violent one?"

He remained seated on the couch, staring at her with his calm, calculated intensity. "No, not that one, Julia. The other one," he said slowly.

She stared at him shakily, trying to piece together, and then it came to her in a rush, the intensity, the wildness, the uncontrollable passion. "The other—" she stammered a bit.

He watched her closely, with little expression, just calmly gauging her reaction. "Yes, we were lovers."

The brandy glass slipped from her fingers, soundlessly bouncing off a dark green throw rug just in front of the sofa. She glanced down at it, hardly recognizing that she'd dropped it. "Oh, I'm sorry," she said distractedly, still wrestling with his unfathomable declaration. "How could that be?"

He stood up, calmly retrieving the glass and placing it on a nearby bookshelf. "You question it?"

She looked at him as though he'd just spoken some indiscernible foreign language. "Yes, it seems, well, perfectly improbable."

He eyed her, she suspected, with a little irritation. "So, you think it is more likely I was the other one — the one that wanted to kill you."

"No, no, of course not," she shook her head. "The whole thing is a fantasy, some sort of strange waking dream. It didn't really happen at all." She said it emphatically, almost enough to convince herself.

He sat down again, looking at her, well, like a psychiatrist trying to analyze some deluded patient. "You really believe this is just some persistent waking dream, as you call it."

She smiled, trying to trivialize it a bit. "Of course, I can't really believe I lived some past life as some Scarlet Ohara southern belle on a huge plantation. I mean, it's ridiculous, right?"

"Ridiculous?"

"Of course, why would you think otherwise? I mean have you ever really remembered past lives?"

He eyed her stoically, "Yes."

She frowned, "No, really."

"Yes, really, and unfortunately, this waking dream, as you call it, is something I share memories of."

She stared at him dumbfounded. He was being so persistent. "What does that mean?"

"I saw myself there in the past as well, with you. Only you were someone else."

"The southern belle?"

"You were someone else's wife, and we," he stopped.

"Were lovers?"

"Yes."

She frowned distinctively, "So, the man who wanted to kill me was probably—"

"Your husband."

She waited for a moment, waited for something, anything, to dig her out of this bizarre circumstance. "Well, that's just impossible."

He stared at her, beginning to smile a bit. "This really makes you uncomfortable."

"I really have no idea what you want me to say, Nicholas."

He smiled a bit more, seeming completely bemused at their predicament. "Yes, I can see that. Well, why don't we just shelve this for the time being? May I ask you something else, Julia?"

She settled down shakily into a small bergere chair a little distance from the sofa. He leaned forward, making her feel even more uncomfortable, if that was possible. "The rest of this waking dream, as you call it — the energy."

"Yes, it was as if there was energy all over me, all over my—"

Then she paused, realizing what she was about to say. "All over your what exactly?"

She sighed deeply. Why was this happening to her now? "I was going to say all over my naked body. That was what I felt — water, then energy pouring all over me."

She glanced up, meeting his eyes. There was no humor there, nothing but scrutiny. "Did you feel like yourself?"

"What does that mean?"

"I mean, could you have tapped into something else? Something that might give us a clue as to the whereabouts."

"Oh yes, of course, the elemental thing." She'd finally caught on. "I, I don't know. It was all tied up in everything else. It's really difficult to separate anything." She touched her head, which now seemed to be curiously aching.

"You're tired."

She straightened up in the rather uncomfortable chair. It was odd how much of the furniture in this time zone was just that — uncomfortable. "I am. It's been a long day."

He stood up, placing his brandy glass on a nearby table. "Then you should rest." Crossing to her, he held out his hand for her, which she took, rising to her feet. "Rest tonight, and we'll sort things out in the morning."

She nodded, turning and trying not to meet his eyes. It was entirely too much to consider, too much to deal with. And after all, what possible impact could some past life have on what was happening now?

Sensory Overload

Chapter Twenty

She stared out the window into the darkness. It was late. Alice had helped her out of the somewhat complicated evening gown some time ago, and into the long white nightgown, she wore now. She'd expected to fall into bed close to total exhaustion, but her eyes never closed. They simply fixed on the ceiling filled with images of a ridiculously overstimulating day. Her mother had called it sensory overload. Even as a young child, for some reason, she had the capacity to short-circuit if there was too much commotion to process in one setting. Aunt Lilia said it had to do with her empathetic nature. She absorbed much more than most people, who would just shut down as a matter of self-preservation. That was something she had never learned effectively, just to shut down.

When she married Peter, there had been nights when she would just be awake roaming their townhouse. At first, it bothered him, but then he learned to ignore it, as he seemed to ignore any aspect of her that displeased him. It was embarrassing as she now looked back on how much control over her life she'd given him. It was difficult for her to understand and more difficult to explain to anyone else. But on those nights, like tonight, she would curl up in a big overstuffed chair by a window downstairs and sit in the darkness wide-eyed — until it passed, which usually took at least a day.

She allowed herself to feel this house. Her senses stretched out in every direction, and all seemed quiet and calm, unlike her distracted, rambling mind. And so, she stood up, grabbed the long ivory shawl she'd worn with her dress earlier in the evening, and set out to find a calming spot within Nicholas Burke's cottage.

She tiptoed into the hallway, which was cast in long, heavy shadows. There was very little light anywhere. Evidently, night lights weren't popular in 1910. Allowing her eyes to adjust, she headed to the stairway, her bare feet connecting with the re-markably cool and smooth wooden floor. She didn't have a clue as to where she was going, just wanting to find some distrac-tion to relieve the anxiety that had seized every inch of her flesh.

As she softly landed on the ground floor, she peered through the semi-darkness. It seemed a little better lit than up-stairs. There was a soft light left on in one of the front rooms. If she were home, she would have taken some aspirin and curled up in front of some late-night TV.

But as it was, she lacked both painkillers and entertain-ment. She thought about the books she'd seen on the bookshelves in Nicholas' study. But her heart clutched a bit at heading in that direction. They'd ended the evening on such an awkward note — her deflecting his inquiries and he being largely silent and oddly reflective. It bothered her immensely. When she came here, it was clear. He'd kidnapped her. She was here against her will. But now, the edges were becoming blurred. It wasn't so unpleasant here, and it wasn't as if she didn't enjoy his company. He was a chameleon, unpredictable — sharp, intelligent, amusing, solicitous, demanding. So many things, she couldn't keep up. And now, he tells her they were once lovers, long ago in another life. In an odd way, that revelation scared her, and in another inexplicable way, it thrilled her. And it was this reaction that disturbed her more than anything. She couldn't lose herself again. She couldn't lose all the ground she'd gained since Peter.

She tried to sweep the thoughts away. It was too much to deal with — all of it, from the visions in the morning to the crazy séance and all the people with all their odd baggage of energy she could feel. Too much — that was exactly why she was prowling this old dark house, trying to find some relief from it all. And then, she remembered that lovely breakfast room at the back of the house overlooking the patio. It had reminded her so much of her sunroom at Solomon Place. And she could sit there, at least for a little while, staring out the windows and being soothed by the energy from it.

Slowly, she began to make her way through the house. It was strangely winding in design, more complicated than one would think at first glance. She was sure there were rooms she had yet to see — the kitchen, quarters for Alice and her mother, and perhaps others. As she passed by his study, her heart clutched for a moment. The door was closed, but there was a light emanating from it. He was awake. She could feel it, feel him within. But she quietly passed by, heading toward her destination. Finally, as much as through sense as memory, she arrived in the breakfast room. Like everywhere else, it largely lay in shadow, but there was enough light from outside, moonlight, to ever so softly illuminate its interior.

Taking one of the table chairs, she positioned it facing the window. She curled up into it, Indian fashion, as she'd done often as a child watching her mother painting her pictures in the sunroom. It was a comforting memory, soothing. She breathed in deeply, trying to calm herself, her heart seeming tied up in some inexplicable anguish. *"Breathing, breathing, my dear, is so important,"* Aunt Lilia had told her. She closed her eyes and concentrated on her breathing, allowing the competing images that had crowded her mind tonight to float away one by one.

It was helping a bit, at any rate. Some of the anxiety was beginning to slip away. She concentrated on herself only, not understanding, not unraveling mysteries present and past — only herself and the immediate energy around her being of a calming, pure nature. And then, just as she was beginning to feel the anxiety drip away, she felt the shift. She was reluctant to open her eyes. She felt herself so close to being in a better place. But there was no help for it.

Nicholas stood across from her in the shadows. He was no longer dressed in the fine tuxedo from earlier in the evening. He was only wearing a loose white shirt and a pair of trousers. "Sorry to interrupt," he said quietly. She felt an instinctive flutter of nervousness rise in her. "Don't," he said softly, "you were doing well."

She uncrossed her legs and brought them back down to the floor. "What do you mean?" she asked, still slightly lulled by the state she'd been achieving seconds before.

"Your meditation, it was helping you. I didn't want to disrupt it."

She sighed, "I don't understand how—"

"How did I know?" He walked closer to her, his features now more discernible in her vision. "In some ways, you're very easy for me to read, to sense your feelings and thoughts, but not in others." He smiled, "Well, it's very complicated. What's keeping you awake?"

"Everything, too much of everything." She pulled the shawl a little tighter around her shoulders, suddenly feeling a bit too vulnerable."

He answered quietly, "I see."

"And you?" she asked impulsively, but then second-guessing herself. Perhaps some doors shouldn't be opened.

He pulled a chair from the table and positioned it directly across from hers, perhaps a foot or two away, then sat in it, staring at her directly through the shadows. "For me, plans gone awry, I suppose. A great teacher of mine told me once my worst flaw was that I overestimated my power to control things, and my second was that I was too impulsive."

"Control and impulsiveness, not the easiest combination," she murmured.

He smiled, "No, they don't tend to mesh."

She looked away, finding his intense scrutiny unnerving. But then he leaned in, lightly touching her chin and turning her face slowly back to him. "I've been wondering something, Julia. Did you like being married at all?"

Her eyes widened at the strange question. "Not much," she murmured.

He slowly let his hand drop but continued to stare at her, probing, "Why?" he asked.

She took a deep breath. "It hurt so much, feeling as though I was not appreciated for who I really was."

"Was he a complete idiot?"

"Nicholas, I—"

And then, he lightly placed his fingertips on her lips to hush her. "I think he must have been to let you slip away. You fascinate me, confound me. How could he possibly want you to be anything but what you are?" She breathed in deeply, her heart thumping wildly. It was so easy, so easy to just sink into the comfort he was offering, but so complicated. "I didn't think you would be like this. I didn't think."

"Impulsive," she murmured.

And then he smiled just before he reached in and started to kiss her, just before he pulled her gently but so fluidly onto his lap and began kissing her again and blotting out of her mind anything that made sense.

A Change of Circumstance

Chapter Twenty-One

It was the darkness again, the shadows, just as it had been the first time he came to her. Julia tried to separate the confusing impressions, some now, some from that other time trying to mix in. Nicholas had pulled both of them to their feet and drew her with him until they'd reached the study. There was a soft glow in the room of one lamp on a distant table. For a moment, just a moment, he'd separated from her to close the door behind him. And it was enough to allow her mind to clear for a second, to think what she was doing. "Wait," she whispered as he returned to her.

But he didn't answer, not with words. His arms were around her again in an embrace, kissing her gently but with persistence. It was muddled. She couldn't think clearly. His touch was mesmerizing, like nothing she could remember. He was kissing her neck, unbuttoning the gown, the high-neck old-fashioned nightgown. Her hands tightened on his shoulders. "Nicholas," she whispered heavily. "This is crazy. We can't do this."

His face was in her hair, brushing against her ear, whispering, "Let go, Julia. This is right."

He was leading her, maneuvering her to the sofa against the wall. Her mind was reeling. It was so easy, so easy to fall into this, into his world — his arms. But a tremor of cold panic seized her as he swept her onto the sofa and pulled his shirt off over his head. This was real. He would be making love to her any moment. She pulled herself up, putting her hand out in front of her. "I can't," she rasped, her voice sounding strange and hoarse in her ears.

He stopped, staring at her. Something odd crossed his face, a recognition that seemed to penetrate the wild storm of passion they were caught up in moments earlier. "What is it?" he asked, breathing heavily. But his hands were on her, on her shoulders, touching her gently as though he needed the contact. "What are you afraid of?" he said, with that undercurrent of determination she'd come to know so well.

She looked away, unable to meet his gaze, to voice what had surfaced in her mind at such an inopportune moment. This was her. She was not made of the stuff of wild romantic moments like this one. Too much had happened. He pulled her into his arms, sitting beside her and pulling her legs across his lap. "Tell me. I can feel that you want this as much as I do, Julia. Need this. What is it?"

"I'm just not good at this." She managed to get out a bit quakily.

He stared at her with concern. He was stroking her arm quietly, her hair. "Open your mind to me," he whispered. "Let me see."

She could feel him holding her, but closer now, next to her thoughts, her feelings. He wanted her to let down her guard so that he could know, but then he would see pain — the intimate kind of pain that couldn't be shared. It was the price that bad marriages extolled on your soul. The kind that was secret, not to be expressed. "Nicholas, you don't understand," she whispered, wanting his comfort, needing it, but at the same time—

"Don't be afraid," he murmured. Then, almost without thought, led by his soothing voice, she relaxed, relaxed against his body, and let go of all the barriers.

It was painful, the collage of flashes. No one could tell you or explain. It was only supposed to be physical. Isn't that what everyone said? But the emotional pull, drain of intimacy with someone who has no real understanding of you, it was like being repeatedly cut and bleeding from the inside. And then in the end, even worse — he didn't care at all what she wanted, what she felt at all. She was his wife, belonged to him. It diminished her, not even having the strength or feeling that she had the right to fight for herself anymore.

He kissed her softly on her hair and her cheek, where she felt tears rolling down. He exhaled deeply as though sharing her knowledge with him had extolled some price. "It won't be like that, Julia. I promise. We're connected. You feel it. Our spirits can help heal each other." Gently, so gently, he kissed her again. "Tell me what you want," he said softly.

She breathed in deeply, hating the ache, the stab of pain she still felt from the past. "I want to stop hurting," she whispered.

He hesitated for a moment as though he was searching her face. And then, as though he'd found something, he acted. He kissed her again, this time with such intensity as though he'd stopped holding anything back. He swept her back in his arms and laid her on the couch. She waited and watched as he undressed, her heart beating wildly with both excitement and fear. It was decided and terrified her, although she was powerless to stop anything. He caressed her face and then pulled the nightgown upward, pulling it over her head and finishing the process of undressing her by removing the rest of her undergarments that this demure time frame had insisted upon. He paused for a moment, staring into her eyes. "I'm still afraid," she whispered.

"As am I," was his reply before he put his hands on her again, and thought fled in a swirl of sensation. They allowed the shadows to sweep around them and guard them protectively as they had done so long ago.

He dreamed, dreamed of long white halls glistening, humming around him, and his footsteps echoing on fine white marble. *"Focus,"* the voices whispered around him. "It's *close,*" they echoed. He walked further, feeling an ache spread throughout his body. And then the light flowed in, blinding light. It was so close, so close, the memories. *"No,"* they echoed around him. *"You haven't earned the knowledge yet."*

His eyes opened in the darkness of Julia's room. She lay beside him, sleeping soundly. He'd brought her here. A flash of vivid memory swept across his mind after he'd made love to her in the study. He stared at her through the shadows. Her pale skin seemed nearly luminescent. She was dazzling. He sighed deeply — controlling and impulsive. All of this being with her, becoming her lover last night, was impulsive but not unexpected. He was not a man who did not consider all possibilities. It had solidified their connection that he'd felt the moment he'd laid eyes on her. He'd felt it even before bringing her here, although he would not allow himself to acknowledge it consciously. He needed something from her. He needed her to lead him to the elemental, and that was where his focus had been until now — until last night when, finally, something snapped, and he gave reign to powerful and clearly uncontrollable emotions.

But there had been another less obvious benefit. He was closer now to the elemental. Through Julia, he could sense its presence. However, locating it was another matter. Again, he glanced at her sleeping form, dark hair framing her lovely face. It was important to set things right now as quickly as possible. Now, he had his own life to consider and how he would convince her to be a part of it. Quietly, he slipped out of the bed, determined not to wake her. He had no idea what time it was, but it was clearly still very early. He pulled on the clothes he'd brought and silently headed down to the study. There were things to consider and plans to be made before they talked again.

Julia felt a chill pass over her skin. She opened her eyes to a room where the early light of dawn was just beginning to make its presence known. She glanced around. The place in the bed beside her was empty, although she remembered him being there last night. At the foot of the bed, her nightgown was draped. Of course, she was chilled. She was entirely naked. She grabbed the gown, quickly straightening it out and pulling it over her head. All she needed was for Alice to barge in and find her without a stitch of clothing on. Of course, if Nicholas was still here, she would probably assume— She stopped herself mid-thought. She would probably assume she'd spent the night with her husband, whom she emphatically reminded herself – *He was not!*

She leaned back in the bed in a bit of disbelief. She'd just slept with her kidnapper. What was that, the Stockholm Syndrome? She'd done it. It was unbelievable, so personal, so intimate, so exciting. She felt keenly as though she'd never done this before. Anything that had gone on between her and Peter paled as though it were some farcical impression of what had happened last night. And this realization, amongst other things, scared her to death.

She was so vulnerable now. He had power over her. She'd held nothing back. And where did that leave them? Her head spun with the recognition of how complicated things had just become and with the dizziness of an unrecognized low blood sugar — of course, too much commotion, unpredictability. No wonder her physical state was completely out of whack.

She swung her legs around again, feeling that familiar sweep of imbalance. She breathed deeply. It was stupid. She didn't have something here. Back home, she always had some food in the room in case it happened — back home that would be standard. But mercifully, there was a light knock on the door, as though angels somewhere were looking out for her. She answered shakily as Alice's welcome sweet face stuck her head in the door. Without allowing her to speak, she quickly said, "I'm not feeling well, Alice. Could you please quickly bring me a glass of juice or something sweet?" The girl's eyes got large as though in recognition, and she quickly disappeared. It was clear that Nicholas had alerted her to this possibility. Already, she began to see a bit of spottiness in her vision. But she braced herself to hold it together until Alice returned. What else could she do?

Within minutes, Alice flew into the room holding a substantial porcelain mug of orange juice, which she gratefully took with trembling hands. It was amazing to her how fast the onset of this hypoglycemic episode had been. But then again, it wasn't the first time she'd awoken to a low blood sugar. Alice hovered over her as she sipped the juice. Slowly, she could feel a measure of control returning to her body, although it was clear she wouldn't be right again unless she ate something. "Alice, why don't you get Julia something to eat? I'll stay with her." She heard Nicholas' voice from somewhere on the other side of the girl.

Alice straightened up, still looking concerned. "I'll be back soon, Miss." And she disappeared.

Glancing up and focusing on something other than the life-saving juice, she realized that a very concerned-looking Nicholas had settled on the bed beside her. She still felt as though most of her was trembling. Without a sound, he slipped his arm around her shoulders. "Is it bad?" he asked.

She nodded, still trying to concentrate on the stabilizing effect of the quick sugar that had just hit her system. She returned it to her lips with a shaky hand that he reinforced with his own. She drank, concentrating on returning to herself, as she felt him lean over and lightly kiss her forehead.

Things were better, she thought. She'd eaten, stabilized her blood sugar, taken several readings that confirmed this, and was helped into a new peach-colored day dress that Alice had helped her put on. It was tailored, fitted, and not even demanding a bustle. And as she looked at her reflection in the mirror, she thought she looked pretty. She wondered how Nicholas would like her in it, and then she abruptly stopped herself. She wanted to please him, and maybe that was what he was counting on. Shadows and insecurities began to traipse across her mind. Perhaps, he wanted her in this position, this vulnerable position, so he could get what he was after. She frowned at her reflection. Well, it's not like she was any closer to leading him to the elemental because of last night. So, sleeping with her didn't really accomplish much of anything except make her more complacent.

She steeled herself. She didn't like this, all these doubts, feeling weak. Whatever Nicholas Burke might think, things had changed here. She checked her appearance once more in the large dresser mirror and then headed out of her room purposefully. As she arrived in the downstairs parlor, she nearly ran headlong into Alice, who appeared to be doing some light cleaning with a feather duster. "Miss Julia," she looked up, a bit surprised.

"Where is Mr. Burke?"

Her eyes widened, "Oh, he's in the study ma'am, but he asked that he not be disturbed unless it was an emergency."

She smiled. "Yes, well, it is. Thank you, Alice," and she skirted around the girl with her astonished expression and headed with bold footsteps to the study. She stopped in front of the closed door, quickly sweeping away the torrid images from the night before. She knew if she stopped to think too much she wouldn't do, well, what she'd decided to. Quite forcibly, she lifted her fist up on the door and knocked, knocking loudly three times. She took a deep breath and waited.

Quite suddenly and jarringly, the door flew open, and Nicholas stood in the frame, looking concerned. He eyed her with a bit of confusion. "Are you all right?" he finally asked.

She drew in a deep breath, steeling herself. "No, not really. Can we talk?"

He stared at her for what seemed like an endless moment, although she knew it probably just lasted a few seconds. Then he stepped back, making a sweeping movement with his hand for her to enter. She stepped within, hearing him closing the door behind them, not so unlike the night before. Again, she quelled the intimate images that surfaced. If she allowed herself to be bogged down with all that emotion, nothing at all would be accomplished.

He walked past her, settling into a chair near the roll-top desk against the wall. He eyed her curiously, "Are you sure you're recovered? You're acting strangely."

She was still standing, just standing in the center of the room, trying to puzzle out the best course of action. "I am fine, physically," she emphasized.

"I see. Then something else is bothering you," he said with some deliberation. "Well, would you care to sit and talk about it?" he continued in a very moderated tone. It was his psychiatrist's voice. She could imagine him using it for any number of unpredictable patients. And she wondered, distractedly, if she could be that to him — some sort of project. He frowned, and she wondered if he was picking up on these thoughts. "Sit down, Julia," he said softly.

She picked a chair, that bergere chair, which was against the wall. The sofa would have been closer to him, but after last night. Well, she didn't really want to deal with the sofa just yet. She caught his gaze from across the room. It wasn't a huge room, not like the parlors, so they weren't leagues away from each other. But just at the moment, it seemed like an awkward distance. "I needed to say a few things."

He watched her carefully, "Not easy to say?" he asked.

"No, I mean, I'm not sure."

"Well, in my experience, it's best just to say it, whatever it is."

She nodded, "Things have changed."

"Undeniably," he said smoothly.

"When I first came here, well, it wasn't my choice."

"I kidnapped you." Her eyes met his. There was no amusement there, just scrutiny, calmly evaluating.

Again, she looked away. It was definitely easier this way. "I didn't have a choice in anything."

"I know that," he said softly.

"You told me what you wanted me to know, which was very little, but now," she hesitated. Yes indeed, what about now?

He stood up and walked over to her, standing in front of her. She couldn't help but look into his eyes. He took her hand in his. "But now, as you've said, things have changed."

"Nicholas," she said with an undeniable tremor in her voice. "Either let me in, let me understand what's really happening, or let me go."

He hesitated, seeming to take a moment to absorb the impact of her words, and then lightly dropped her hand, walking across the room. His back was to her for some time before he finally turned around — a different expression on his face, one undeniably of determination. "Yes, that's only fair. Well, it's not an easy or uncomplicated story. So, settle in and I'll tell you all about it, all about the elemental."

The Story of the Elemental

Chapter Twenty-Two

He sat on the edge of the sofa, their sofa, and was quiet for a moment, seeming as though he needed to collect his thoughts. But Julia just waited, she felt it in her skin, in her veins, how profound and difficult a moment this was for him. For some reason, Nicholas was not a very trusting man. He depended on himself and fought hard to be in control of his world. But to relinquish, to let that control escape a bit, was taking a risk, a terrible risk that could prove to be incredibly advantageous or completely disastrous. So, she waited patiently.

"This goes back Julia, back to another time, even before that past life we spent together." He cleared his throat. "In the early 1500s, there was a famous philosopher, scientist," and then he eyed her curiously, "alchemist named Philippus Aureolus Paracelsus. Are you familiar with the name?" he asked.

She searched her mind. Paracelsus seemed to ring a distant bell, but she couldn't quite connect it. She shook her head, "I'm not sure."

"He lived long ago, actually during the Renaissance. He wrote quite a bit and studied many things—among them invisible beings that exist in other dimensions, dimensions that run very close to ours."

"Elementals?" she murmured.

"Yes, elementals, he described in detail their existence, pure beings, composed and fueled by energy. Those fueled by fire were called salamanders, by earth gnomes, by water undines, and by air sylphs. Some know them as nature spirits. Many cultures and religions revere them in different ways. The American Indians believed that all things contained spirits."

"And you're saying this is real."

"I'm saying that what we see is not all there is. Many things, many creatures exist in nearly the same space with us, just a fraction of a dimension off but close enough for us to feel them, not only elementals but other things—some parasites, some that actually feed off of our energy." He shook his head. "I digress. It was Paracelsus' contention that to become ruler over the elemental was to achieve great power, the power of a magician or a necromancer."

She grimaced, "That doesn't sound good."

He sighed, "Yes, and there was another man. He was not so renowned but ambitious, perhaps more ambitious than his Master Paracelsus. While Paracelsus understood the existence of and wrote about the elementals, he respected the line drawn between science and God's work. But the other man—" he paused.

"He didn't."

He shook his head, "He was eager to make a name for himself, to experience the power Paracelsus spoke of. So, he built on the work of his teacher, and he used his science to draw the elemental into our dimension and subdue it."

She stared at him a bit wide-eyed. She remembered the dream, the dream of the old man with the blue eyes. "It suffers," she whispered.

He looked at her with confusion. "How do you know that?"

She shook her head. "I dreamed about an old man. The room was so white. And he told me."

He nodded, "Yes, to be torn from its natural state made it suffer greatly. But you have to understand, they are not like us at all. Their life force lasts thousands of years. It was painful, but it survived. And it did more than that. It touched him, his mind, his heart. It is a pure energy, pure feeling. It changed him, making him understand his mistake. But it was too late."

"Why, why didn't he just send it back?"

He shook his head, "He couldn't. It wasn't possible. So, instead, he vowed to protect it until he could find a way to return its life to it."

She swallowed painfully. It sounded like a fairy tale of some kind. It couldn't be true, yet here she'd encountered two men turning over heaven and earth to find a thing that couldn't exist. She thought of the dreams, the buzzing, the energy pouring over her. It did feel real, but it couldn't be. "I don't understand. Christian, when he talked about it, called it the Dubourg crystal."

At the mention of Christian's name, a darkness seemed to pass over his face. He stood up and walked across the room, then turned around and faced her, his expression steeled. "It's been hundreds of years since the elemental was trapped in our world. Much information has been put out about it—some true, some subterfuge in an effort to shield it."

"He said it was something that belonged to his family."

"It seems he is distantly related to the original alchemist who captured the elemental. His name was Claude Treme."

She leaned back in the chair, trying to piece together what he'd told her. "So, he wants to find it."

"For its power. He's not the first. Treme left journals, writings, accounts of his work. Some of it is true, some of it deliberately crafted lies. No one knows everything. As I've told you, he was changed by it, his heart. And he pledged his life to protect it. It's a karmic debt."

His words resonated in her mind, "Karmic?" she asked.

"Yes," he answered softly.

"And, now I know everything except about you, Nicholas. I don't understand your connection here."

"Treme's actions were an abomination against nature, against spirit, perhaps God," his voice sounded so cold. "That kind of debt does not go unpaid." She wondered now if she'd made a mistake here, made a mistake in demanding the truth. The truth comes with its price, with its obligation, and its burdens. "I told you that I did remember past lives."

"Yes, the life we shared."

"And other ones," his voice sounded oddly distant and ominous in her ears. She knew it, of course, before he said it, but until he did, it wouldn't make it real — wouldn't obligate her to the burden of finally understanding. "It's my obligation, Julia, my karmic debt that I've carried from lifetime to lifetime. I was Claude Treme. It was my sin that trapped that innocent creature in the hell that it now enjoys."

The room was silent as his words wrapped around her like a cold mist. *"It was my sin that trapped that innocent creature in the hell that it now enjoys."* She breathed deeply — her head feeling as though it were in a complete swirl from everything he had told her. But now that he had finished his story, he was silent. He was waiting, waiting, she felt perhaps for her to be horrified, to throw all of this back into his face, or perhaps not really knowing exactly what kind of reaction to expect. But of course, all of this was lifetimes ago. Who knew what kind of things she'd done in past lives, what karma she may have incurred. But it was overwhelming, something of this magnitude that after hundreds of years, he still felt bound to it, still obligated to set things right.

"I don't understand," she said with amazing calm that even surprised her. "If you were Claude Treme, then why can't you find the elemental? He would be the one who would know where to look."

The air felt thick with tension and emotion, as though in explaining this to her, he'd released a Pandora's Box that had unleashed all the ills upon their formerly innocent world. She felt now that there was some truth in the adage, *Ignorance is Bliss.* "Yes, you would think so. But the memories of that for me are selective. It seems I've had to earn every scrap of knowledge concerning this. Perhaps part of it is my penance. Perhaps it has been blocked by others seeking the same thing. I can't really say. But you, you have been the only solid lead I've been able to find."

She looked at him with confusion. "I still don't understand that. What connection could I have to this?"

He looked at her intently with the slightest mark of desperation. "I'm not sure, Julia. So far, the only connection that I can deduce is that you have a connection to me."

She stared at him, marking a degree of desperation on his face. If she left now, then all his hope of rectifying this karmic debt would be lost. She felt bewildered. What now? Where to go from here? "How long have you known about this?"

He answered slowly. It seemed as though explaining this to her had taken quite a bit of energy out of him. "Abstractly, since I was very young, in dreams, flashes of vision. But concretely, not until I was much older when I studied with masters in India and other places. They helped me discover the truth of it all. You see, I could go on with my life, not addressing this, but for me, it would be a torment. We all have a spiritual path, an ascent of evolution, that our spirits climb. But this matter, what I did is like a roadblock, or perhaps in some unforeseen way, it's my opportunity to learn. But essentially, I am stuck. I can't move forward unless I set things right."

She heard the pain in his voice at that final proclamation. For someone like him, who had developed his psychic and other abilities to the magnitude that enabled him to bring not only himself but her as well through time, she could only imagine what a great torment recognizing this must be to him. "I can see why it's so important to you, Nicholas. I mean, you went to the trouble to bring me here because of it."

He stood in front of her, face stoic but intense. "I need your help, Julia. I can't do this without you."

Here was the moment now that she'd known was coming once she learned the truth — her decision, her choice. And it came more naturally than she'd expected. She didn't think, didn't consider the consequences, didn't weigh much of any-thing. She just answered in the only way she could. "Of course, of course, I will help you."

Something passed over his features, and the light returned to his eyes. He took both of her hands, lifted her to her feet, and pulled her into a tight embrace. With just that contact, she could feel all the anxiety seep out of her. There was possibility now. Perhaps they could do this and when it was done. But she stopped herself. She couldn't think beyond the present. Things were too complicated now. She pulled out of the embrace, look-ing at him intently. "But what do we do? The séance didn't yield much in the way of results."

He shook his head, his features looking more animated, less dour, as though in explaining the story to her and obtain-ing her cooperation he'd somehow lightened the burden he'd been carrying. "I don't know if that's entirely true. I think we should go back to it and take a closer look."

"Go back?" she asked with confusion. "How is that possible?"

"I want to hypnotize you again."

Now this she hadn't anticipated. She frowned explicitly, "And that worked out so well the first time."

"It's different now. We're both seeking the same thing."

She felt a bit of inexplicable trepidation coiling around somewhere inside her. "All right, if you think so," she agreed somewhat hesitantly.

He smiled broadly, then lifted her chin, kissing her with a very soft brush of a kiss that reminded her of all the other things they'd shared now. "Yes, it's time to get all of this settled," he murmured before he kissed her again, not nearly so innocently.

Retreading Old Steps

Chapter Twenty-Three

There was no reason for it. Things had taken an amazingly positive turn. He had told Julia the worst of things, yet she had still committed to help him. The one person he needed the most right now had vowed to stay at his side. In some ways, he was astonished. For him, life never worked out this way. He'd always known that he'd often taken unorthodox turns along his path and was not what you would call a particularly scrupulous man in his methods. And for such actions, there was always a price to pay. Life did not run smoothly.

So, while he was happy he no longer had to play the role of the adversary with Julia, another part of him was waiting—waiting for the other side to rear its ugly head.

"Do you really think going back over this again will do any good?" she asked.

They were upstairs in his office. She was seated just on the edge of the chaise lounge, outfitted in her peach-colored dress. Her face looked focused, very determined, and he wondered with distraction if he'd really earned this degree of loyalty on her part. He thought back to the night before and, more than anything wanted to scoop her up in his arms and renew the passion that had touched them both so profoundly. He wanted to just leave behind other obligations, other concerns, and focus solely on each other. Was it selfish? He wondered. But then again, who was he, and what sort of future could he expect if he did not atone for the past?

"I think it's where we need to start," he said in response to her question. She nodded, smiling a bit tremulously. She was nervous for some reason. He could tell. Again, his mind considered the other side of things. There is always the yin and yang of the universe — the light and the chaos he'd been told. There must be balance, and balance sometimes comes at great cost.

"Just lie back," he responded, now wholly focusing on the task at hand. "And listen to my voice. I will guide you." She closed her eyes, and he focused his mind on the journey they were about to take. He relinquished his dark, foreboding thoughts with the recognition that whatever was to come would do so, and he would deal with it when it did.

It was odd. There was a different feeling now as she began to travel. She could hear Nicholas' voice in her mind, strong, direct, guiding tones but comforting. She wasn't trying to block him now, and it opened up wide new vistas. Again, as before, they were arriving at Josephine Delachaise's mansion. She watched as Nicholas first stepped down from the carriage and then took her hand, guiding her out. She wasn't in her own body. She was watching as though she were two different people. "This is something," she murmured to herself.

"Stay focused," was his response, and then she looked to the side, seeing a slight impression of Nicholas next to her.

"You're here with me," she said.

"Yes, but it's a tenuous connection we have right now. Follow where you are drawn. It's important."

She moved behind their other selves as they were ushered into the enormous house. But it was different for her this way. She could see energy everywhere. Everything around them was giving off energy, albeit not always positive. Various objects — paintings, a mahogany curule chair, an ornate giltwood mirror — were seeping red, red energy. Her Aunt Lilia had always told her that objects absorb the energy around them, and some can become nearly impossible to cleanse.

As the other Julia and Nicholas waited in the foyer, she swept ahead, drawn to the parlor where Josephine had congregated with her guests. They were all there: the Dugreys, Francisca Maxwell, Benjamin, and Anne Lamarque. For some reason, seeing this last couple sent a curious chill into her. What was it about them that was so odd, other than the disparity in their ages and the fact that Anne Lamarque looked like a terrified little sheep? "Focus," she heard Nicholas' voice coaxing.

"What possible bearing could they have on—"

"I don't know," he responded, "but there is a reason for everything."

Reluctantly, Julia moved closer to them and felt a strange sort of breathlessness as she approached. It was almost as though the atmosphere had become denser around the couple. She concentrated harder, trying to see what exactly was amiss. Then it came to her. Anne Lamarque barely had any aura of energy. As she concentrated, she could see it ever so faintly around her body, mostly a soft yellow hue. And then she noted Benjamin Lamarque, standing there smug, conversing with Louis Dugrey. Just momentarily, he slipped his arm around Anne, lightly touching her, and Julia could see it — energy slipping out of Anne, being drawn into him, into his great gray-colored aura.

"What is this?" she nearly hissed.

"He's a drainer."

"A what?" she asked.

"This is complicated, Julia."

"This is horrible, Nicholas. What exactly are you saying?"

"It's an evolutionary state of the spirit. We've all been through it, lived lives as drainers. It's where the myth of the vampire comes from. A drainer actually draws spiritual energy from another person. And the closer they are, the more they draw."

"Closer?"

"More connected, more intimately connected."

"Oh," she murmured, "so we've all been like him."

"Not exactly. A drainer has to learn that they can't evolve by using or taking from another. It's a difficult lesson. Some just refuse to learn it for some time and revel in its power. Like Mr. Lamarque here, his aura isn't that muddied shade of gray for no reason."

"His poor wife."

"Yes, it is sad. She clearly is under his complete control."

She breathed deeply, watching the other Julia and Nicholas enter the room. Benjamin Lamarque's eyes were on her, watching with interest. It was disturbing. Something was there, something peculiar. She remembered him grabbing her hand during the séance and her repulsion so strongly that it felt like a burn. But she knew there was something to discover, so she moved closer to him, trying to feel. "Be careful," she heard Nicholas' voice in her mind. But this was why she was here, to uncover the truth. She was beside Lamarque now, and she opened her mind to impressions from him.

The thoughts hit her painfully. People exist at different vibrations of energy, her Aunt Lilia had told her, sort of like frequencies. The more evolved you are, the higher the frequency, and the less evolved you are, the lower the frequency. That is why there are some people that it is simply impossible for you to connect with or reach in any way. They literally exist on a different level.

She hadn't really understood this until she was hit with a wave of thought from Benjamin Lamarque's mind. It was painful to field them, and she could only describe it as coarse, being hit with shards of coarseness. "You need to stop," she heard Nicholas' voice distantly.

The man operated on a basic level: greed, envy, and ego—disdain for his lovely wife, which he'd unconsciously drained to the point of having very little left to gain from her. He could sense energy, though, smell it at a nearly primal level. That was why he was so focused on her. She radiated a powerful energy that oddly felt familiar to him.

"Julia," Nicholas' voice.

"Just one minute, I'm close," she answered.

It was her energy, Julia's energy specifically, that reminded him of something. She waited, then dug deeper, something powerful.

"Yes, Sir," she made the voyage well-protected.

She heard the voices in his mind.

"I should hope so, considering what I paid. No damage."

"No sir, in perfect condition. No one would ever know she's quite as old as she is."

"Where did you want her, sir?"

"In the garden, I've erected a special place of honor."

Julia pushed and pushed through, feeling acutely the energy she was losing in doing so. She didn't want to think about whether somehow Benjamin was taking it from her. She just needed to see now. Her inner vision pushed hard against one last barrier, and she was suddenly outside — outside in the daylight in a lovely courtyard. She felt all semblance of breath leave her and felt herself tremble in complete awe. It was simply a fountain, a lovely old-fashioned fountain, but at its heart was a statue made of some sort of strange coppery or brass metal. The statue was a beautiful woman in a Grecian gown, her hands gracefully stretched upward, delicate fingers intertwining, reaching for the sky. Her heart clutched as she could see the lights swirling around the exquisite statue, the fractured energy still seeping from within. Of course, he could feel it, Benjamin Lamarque, but it was limited what he could take. This energy was too pure for him for such a coarse man to assimilate. But he could feel it, feel its power.

"Oh God, Nicholas," she exclaimed, her very last thought just before she was yanked, yanked somewhere else.

The impact hit her directly across the jaw, a physical impact. A beat later, her heart remembered to clutch in fear. Philippe stood over her in rage. "Do you really think you could get away with this? Get away with this betrayal, Ovelia? You belong to me."

There was blood, blood that she tasted in her mouth. She could feel the anger in him, coursing uncontrollably through him. He was going to kill her, and she would never see Antoine again. She scrambled on the bed away from him, but he lurched forward and grabbed her by the shoulders. She screamed as he grabbed a fistful of her hair and yanked her neck back fiercely.

Then, all swirled again into total darkness as she hit the hard cement in front of the St. Louis Cathedral in Jackson Square.

Home Again

Chapter Twenty-Four

It was hot. The pavement was nearly scorching against her cheek. Of course, she could not remember ever having her face directly plastered to it before. And then she felt hands on her, on her arms, trying to lift her.

Her eyes blinked open painfully, the brightness all around her actually piercing her vision. Then she was abruptly dragged up to a sitting position, and a familiar yet oddly unwelcome face peering into hers. "Are you all right, Julia?" He asked in his crisp English accent. And her heart sank. She was back, back to the moment Nicholas had originally taken her.

Her head throbbed. Her vision was hazy, and she felt as though she was going to heave all over Christian Montamat. "Not really," she murmured shakily.

He was crouching down directly in front of her, and she had to admit he did look concerned. "What happened? You were just standing there, and then you collapsed!"

She looked away from his disturbing gaze. Oddly, she couldn't remember having thought so before, before, and then a rush of vivid memories crowded her mind — before Nicholas had taken her to another time. "Weak spell, I think," she answered shakily.

He frowned, and then she could feel him, feel him trying to read her thoughts. And a panic fluttered through her. But there was some problem now, some confusion and fog lying between their minds. He looked intensely bothered by it, frustrated. "Please, Christian, could you take me home? I'm not feeling well at all."

There was a hesitation, and then he nodded, helping her to her feet. It was so strange now. His very touch suddenly chilled her in a way that it hadn't before, reminding her vividly of another time. "My camera," she murmured.

He scooped the case up, which had landed some yards away from her. She wondered if it still worked. It had hit the pavement hard, as had she.

"Is it your blood sugar?"

Julia looked around the house, just as she'd left it that morning so long ago. But for her, so much had happened, so much time had passed, and she didn't feel the same. "I don't think so," she nearly whispered, still so caught up in her impressions. Was it possible, in any way possible, that everything had been a delusion, a vision brought on by a head trauma? That it had been all in her imagination?

"Can I get you anything?" His voice was becoming insistent, aggravating to her. She didn't want him here, not in the least. She needed time alone to puzzle things out. She turned to face Christian Montamat, the man she knew was after the elemental for his own purposes, so implied very selfish purposes. At least, that was what Nicholas had told her — her lover, the man she was now wondering if she had simply made up. "I'm sorry, Christian, about this, about things getting sidetracked this way," she chose her words carefully. "But now, I think perhaps it might be for the best."

An odd expression crossed his face, one she decided instantly she didn't like — one of focus, one of suspicion, and steely determination. All of that wrapped up in one expression on his very British face. "For the best, you say?" he answered in a low voice.

She smiled, at least as much as she could muster, given the awkwardness of the moment compounded with the aches and pains that still plagued her from her spill on the pavement. "Yes, I think really I'm not the person to help you now. As you probably have noticed, I'm dealing with some significant health issues, and frankly, it's all a bit too much for me now. I'm sure you can understand that."

There was a rather long beat before he responded, leading her to question if, indeed, he was even willing to try to understand this. But finally, a bit of the polish she remembered from their initial encounters seemed to return to his manner, and he answered smoothly, "Well, what is clear is that you are quite shaken now and might need some time to recover. But I will ask that once you're feeling more yourself that, I may be permitted to revisit these issues."

Clearly, the man who won't take no for an answer, but she was tired, befuddled, and in no mood to argue. She'd simply have to convince him of the finality of things later. "Well, let's see how it goes."

He nodded slightly, but she could tell he was less than satisfied. "Of course, do get some rest, Julia." He tacked on as she led him out the house. When he finally walked out, she gratefully closed the door behind him. Her head was throbbing, her stomach nauseous, and she felt absolutely feverish, not unlike— And then she remembered the first time she traveled through time when she was so ill. So, if it hadn't happened at all, why would she feel similarly now? Granted, this was not quite the same severity of illness, but the symptoms weren't so very different. Her stomach churned with pain, and she wondered if she should eat or just go throw up. But perhaps this was good, some proof she wasn't delusional. But then, why had she come back now?

A foreboding swept over her, eclipsing the symptoms of illness. She remembered seeing the statue in Benjamin Lamarque's courtyard. The statue that somehow imprisoned the elemental, and just before everything had changed, she called out to Nicholas — Nicholas, who was beside her through most of the journey. Was it possible, and it pained her even to consider it, that she'd found it for him, so he no longer had a use for her? Was that why she was back now? But then another image swept into her mind, another image of violence from the past. It chilled her even beginning to remember. That man, her husband, yanking back her head and even in her mind that awful grating noise, horrible internal breaking of bones in one snap.

Her head swirled, and she headed to the bathroom. She was sick now, her body sick, and sick from the image she recalled. It was too much even to begin to sort through now.

Something was off. Christian left Julia's house feeling disorientated. It didn't mesh. This morning, he had obtained her cooperation, and he felt confident she would lead him to the Dubourg Crystal. But after she'd fainted, it was as if everything shifted. She was different, not accessible to him. And he felt strangely different as well, confused, almost in a fog. Thoughts and feelings were attempting to bleed into his mind, but they didn't quite fit and were out of sync here. As he got into his car, he struggled to clear his mind. He would sort this out one way or another. And then, when that was done, they would find the crystal. He simply wouldn't accept anything else.

She slept, slept heavily, and dreamed of the water. She could feel it flowing over her, cleansing away that darkness that threatened to engulf her. It wasn't really thoughts, not thoughts as we can articulate, but rather something higher, impressions that radiated outward. And there was the energy, the lovely expanding energy, and the hope for peace. For some reason, it was closer now, closer than it had ever been.

Julia opened her eyes in her room. There was still light streaming through the gauzy bedroom shears. She sat up in her bed and took in the familiar furnishings surrounding her. But oddly, it didn't cheer her. How many times while she was away had she hoped desperately to come home, but not now? Now, she wished for the familiarity of the bedroom in Nicholas' Creole cottage. In some strange way, she had grown attached to it. She breathed deeply, feeling a pain stab at her heart that was not physical. She couldn't admit to herself what or rather who she was really attached to. Because the way things were, it was highly probable she would never see him again.

A shadowed corner across the room shifted, and Julia's Great Aunt Lilia moved toward her. Just that moment, she realized tears were streaming down her face. Her aunt's normally placid features had melted into an expression of concern and compassion.

Julia shook her head, trying to stave off the pent-up emotion that was threatening to overtake her now. "Why has everything become such a mess?" she asked in a shattered voice.

Her aunt moved beside her, "Because that is the nature of life here on earth. It breaks us down and then restores us in extraordinary ways."

Sealing Alliances

Chapter Twenty-Five

Pain, pain as he could only describe it, seared through his head. His hands trembled, and the limp body of his now-deceased wife slipped onto the bed. The flesh he touched was still warm, but life had left her, or rather, he had driven it out. He breathed in raggedly. And the pain throbbed inside his head as though something had burst inside.

It was over. But all he felt was empty now, hollow. He'd expected — and his hands continued to tremble as moments before they had been an instrument of execution. He had expected some glint of satisfaction. They'd hurt him. She'd hurt him, but there was nothing — just cold, just quiet.

And then, distantly, he heard a rattling, a heavy pounding. And the bedroom door flew open. He was still dazed, sitting on the bed with his dead wife in his arms. And Antoine stared at him with eyes filled with horror and then rage.

Christian opened his eyes from the meditation. It was so clear now. It had never been this way, just fractured elements, but his heart still beat frantically—his hands trembled. He felt completely drained, completely confused. There were flashes, phantoms of memories from here that lingered but didn't fit anywhere. There were flashes of focusing on this past life, sinking into the feeling of that man—that man that now repulsed him.

Again, he cleared his mind, pulling away from that horrible vision. Instead, he focused on a calmer place, a life he'd spent in the service of God. And he called on his friend, his guide, to help him sort out this strange dilemma.

Her first day back had passed. She'd slept quite a bit, monitored her health, and eaten some, but she essentially walked around in a fog. She tried not to think about what had happened. Just now, her mind couldn't deal with it, and her heart. Well, she definitely didn't want to venture in that direction. So, she focused on the basics.

And today Julia had to try to pick up the pieces of her life. There were some projects, and sketches she had to finish. She did have a life here and had to pay the bills. But it was difficult. She was literally walking around like a shell, gutted of motivation, emotion, and interest in much of anything. Unfortunately, it reminded her hauntingly of that dark time after her marriage broke up with Peter, after her parents had died. She'd been a wreck, falling into a hole of depression until her great aunt had appeared to her and essentially rescued her. She couldn't let that happen again. Whatever was to come, she had to be master of herself.

She took a deep breath, poured herself a second cup of coffee, and headed to the sun porch to do some work. It was eight o'clock in the morning. This was a nice time of day, not hot yet, and the birds were flocking around her mother's granite fountain in the yard.

Her eyes were drawn involuntarily to that fountain. An ache went through her heart as she thought of the other fountain she'd seen in Benjamin Lamarque's courtyard. It wasn't because of her feelings for Nicholas and his need to atone for the past. It was something else. The empathy, the keen empathy she felt for this creature of light, to be trapped in an alien place without comfort and clothed in that strange metal. Somehow, it reminded her of Persephone, being dragged into the Underworld. It pained her, the unfairness of it.

She looked down at the sketch she was making and impulsively flipped the page. She could see it clearly in her mind: the maiden with her hands stretched toward the heavens. So, she began to sketch, sketching with her heart, with her inner vision, what she had seen.

By the time she finished, an hour had passed. She looked down at the drawing, a bit mystified by what she saw. There was so much detail, more so than she usually used. The surroundings and the courtyard had changed somewhat in her picture from what she remembered. She breathed in deeply, realizing that this was not the elemental back then in 1910. This was her now, now in a different courtyard, but still here in the city. But if this were true, that would mean that Nicholas hadn't— Her mind hesitated at his name as she felt a familiar shift in energy.

Slowly, her eyes lifted back to her mother's fountain outside on the patio. And her heart clutched. He was standing there next to it, looking somber, eyes on her. She should be angry. She should immediately demand a thousand explanations from him. But emotions, powerful emotions, took over, and tears began to stream down her face. Almost involuntarily, she unlocked and opened her mother's French doors, where she waited for him. In less than seconds, he'd crossed the ground, ascended the steps, and crushed her into his arms. She didn't have a chance to speak because she was too busy kissing him passionately.

She had never considered herself a particularly romantic or particularly passionate person. Even before her marriage with Peter, she wasn't one to let herself be swept up in things. In some ways, she blamed it on her health, always needing to be vigilant, always needing to be in control. But here, now, feeling desperate relief flood through her at Nicholas' embrace, she felt as though she were caught up in a whirlwind.

"What happened? How did you?"

He'd closed the doors behind them and just continued to hold and kiss her with no restraint. "Later," he muttered, clearly as caught up in the moment as she was. "Where's your room?" he whispered in her ear.

It was crazy, and it was wonderful. "It's upstairs," she indicated through the doorway. And in the next breath, she was swept up in his arms and carried with intent in that direction.

A cool breeze swept across the hillside near the monastery. Flashes of the lifetime he once lived here cascaded across his mind. It had been a fruitful time for him, one of reflection and healing. Sometimes, simplicity and living outside of the world help you put things in their proper perspective.

Gregory sat next to him on the hillside, patiently waiting. He'd often noticed that his old friend and now his guide never offered information, just answered. Although sometimes somewhat cryptically, questions were asked of him. "It seems as though something is wrong with my memory."

"How so?"

"I remember things, but then there are phantom memories, impressions."

"Can you account for it?" he asked with no emotion.

"I'm not sure. But it seems to be centered around Julia Moreau."

"Yes, she seems to be a point of contention with you."

"I'm not sure what that means."

"Perhaps it's time to move on, Christian. Pursuing this matter will not get you what you want."

"It's important I recover the Dubourg crystal."

"Why?"

"Because it belongs to my family."

"Ownership? It's a shaky proposition. Do we really ever own anything, possess anything? You know this thing you seek has a will, a life force. How can you really own something that is alive?"

He shrugged, "You can own a pet."

Gregory laughed softly, "Is that what you think this is, a pet?"

He shook his head, "I don't know."

"Well, you should consider this before you act. Consider what you are doing and what repercussions it will have. There are ways to recover your phantom memories. But be sure of what you really want before you proceed."

"You think I shouldn't?"

"I think there are lessons in everything, my old friend, lessons and consequences."

Julia pulled on a light, silky robe, and Nicholas smiled at her with an intensity that made her blush. "You know, I don't mind if you leave that off."

He was lying in her bed, propped up on one arm, although under the covers, completely naked. "I'm cold," she murmured.

He reached for her, "Come back here. I'll keep you warm."

She curled up on the edge of the bed in her short, silky robe, feeling although his offer was more than tempting, they needed to clear a few things up. "I was afraid I'd never see you again."

"You really didn't think I'd leave you here alone."

"I didn't know what to think. One minute, I was with you, and the next."

He leaned back on the pillow. "You missed a step."

She looked at him with confusion, and then her mind floated back. She saw the fountain, and then she was back at the other place— "the plantation," she murmured.

"What you did was risky, Julia. You found what we were looking for, but you made yourself terribly vulnerable in the process. You were so depleted of energy that it made you accessible."

"Accessible? What does that mean?"

He rolled onto his side and took her hand. "This is so complicated. Ever since I brought you to 1910, someone has been trying to find a way to bring you back."

"Someone?"

He nodded, "He's been using this past life, the intense horrific emotion, to pull your spirit there. This last time, he nearly succeeded, so I did the only thing I could: the safest thing for you. I sent you back."

She shook her head, "I don't understand. How could this person do that, just pick some random past life of mine?"

He sighed deeply, "Nothing is random, Julia. Remember I told you we shared that life? Well, we were not the only ones there. He was there as well, and he used it to manipulate you."

Again, flashes of violence cascaded across her mind. "You don't understand. The last thing I saw was myself being killed. This man, my husband back then, snapping my neck."

He squeezed her hand tighter, his eyes dark with concern and other indiscernible emotions. "I'm so sorry you had to see that."

"So, who is he?" she asked, feeling a mounting well of upset.

"You already know who he is, Julia." His eyes held hers intensely, and the horror of acknowledgment flooded over her.

"You're talking about Christian."

"Yes, Christian Montamat."

The Quest Continues

Chapter Twenty-Six

There were several threads of memory that he was able to re-cover. There was the surface memory — yesterday's events of bringing Julia to the French Quarter, her collapse, and return-ing her home. And there was a phantom thread, days of disorientation, recognizing his memory had been tampered with, and then trying to retrieve Julia by focusing on a past life. That set of recollections was more like a misty dream. But what was clear was that Julia had changed somehow, somewhere around the time of her collapse. Her energy had changed, not to mention her receptivity toward finding the Dubourg crystal. It was as if she had simply closed the door on him. Something or someone had gotten to her.

Christian lay back on his bed in the hotel suite. He didn't begin to understand how all this was done. But the culprit was more than clear — Dr. Nicholas Burke. He felt a degree of des-peration surrounding these contrivances as well. It wasn't clean, wasn't well-planned, nor put together seamlessly. Oth-erwise, there would be no bleed of memories. What was done was done in a rush. And that spoke volumes to him. It was more than clear that Dr. Burke had found something and was scram-bling to secure it before anyone else.

He closed his eyes, concentrating on recharging himself before he made his next move. But it had to be soon. Time was clearly running out.

Her mother called it the Scarlett-O'Hara syndrome — the inability to deal with certain things, aka "problems," and the willingness to put off dealing with the said problem until tomorrow or, in her case, indefinitely. The complication or rather bombshell realization that Christian Montamat, the Englishman who had been lurking around her, ingratiating himself to her, was actually someone that she knew in a former life — who, more specifically, had been her husband who had murdered her. Well, that fell into the category of problems she would prefer dealing with in the next millennium. She had dressed, albeit for the second time this morning, and come downstairs to make coffee.

She heard Nicholas' footsteps as he approached her, slipping his hands around her waist.

"I mean, really?" she blurted out impulsively.

"Really what?" he whispered into her ear."

"Really, you think he was this murderous husband from the past?"

He expertly but slowly spun her around to face him. He'd dressed as well. She hadn't really taken in much detail of his attire when she first saw him. Emotions had erupted so quickly. He was no longer in 1910 garb. He was wearing an off-white button-down shirt and khaki pants — kind of modern, kind of nondescript.

"Yes."

"Yes, what?"

"Yes, I believe Christian Montamat was the husband from the past. It gave him leverage to disrupt you."

"The husband? Don't you mean my husband?"

"I don't like to think about it that way."

She frowned, "Well, do you think he's a threat now?"

"It's harder to murder people today and get away with it."

"Well, that's comforting."

She pulled away from him to get coffee mugs out of the cabinet.

"I like your house," he murmured. "It's filled with energy."

She glanced around for a moment. She hadn't really thought of it that way. Perhaps that was what she found so comforting about the house, besides its pleasant memories. "So, what do we do about this? I tried to put him off, but he's bound to come around again."

He took the mug of coffee she'd handed him, sitting at her breakfast table. "Probably."

She sat across from him, suddenly aware that this solemn shift in his mood went much deeper than Christian Montamat. "What is it?"

He shook his head, looking at her with a very dark expression. "I never expected this to happen, Julia. I always thought that once I found it, I would be able to use everything I had studied over the years of alchemy of transmutation of spiritualism to free her." Then he shook his head, "But I couldn't."

The import of his words trickled in slowly. "You saw her, the elemental?"

"After you were gone, I went to Benjamin Lamarque's house. They weren't home, but I managed to make my way through the gates to the courtyard you had seen. It was just as you had told me. I saw the statue that she was sealed in so long ago—the disguise I had given her as protection during my life as Claude Treme."

His voice faded off as though he were deep in thought. "What happened when you found her?" she asked, not being patient enough for him to begin again.

"It was just like you said," he smiled. I've never actually gotten my hands on Claude Treme's journals, though I have tried. But from the trickles of information that I know of them, he took great pains in sending out red herrings to protect her. That was how the rumor of the crystal got started. There is no crystal, and she isn't a sylph from the air, as he indicated. She belongs to the water. She is an undine."

"The fountain, the water," she murmured, remembering her visions of water pouring all over her.

"Yes, always connected to the water."

She glanced up. He'd stopped again. "What happened?"

"I was, just as you had said, in awe. I could feel the energy emanating so strongly even after hundreds of years from the statue. And then I tried, I tried everything I could to free her." He shook his head slowly. "But nothing worked. And finally, I sent my mind, my thoughts, out to her and the only thing I could interpret coming back from her was — *not the way*."

"Not the way?" she asked. "What does that mean?"

"I don't know. That's all I could get. I hit a brick wall. It's over."

She looked at him with astonishment. "What does that mean? You're giving up?"

He stared at her with confusion as though her words were nonsensical. "I have tried everything I know. I have spent years working on this, preparing for this, and nothing works, Julia."

She sat there feeling the hollowness of defeat in his voice, the devastation. He'd spent so much time trying to set things right. "Well, I don't think you should give up yet Nicholas. I haven't tried. You said this elemental is connected to me some-how. Let me try to reach her."

He stared at her blankly, "We don't even know where she is. I found her nearly ninety years ago. She could be anywhere now."

She shook her head, "No, no, she's in the city. I felt it when I was with Christian. We'll find her, and I'll try."

He looked at her with more concern than skepticism. "You don't know what you're getting into here, Julia. What could happen."

She smiled at the evident caring she heard in his voice. She recognized how very much she liked hearing it there. "That's never stopped you."

Another look passed over his face, one she sneakingly thought might be admiration. "Yes, I suppose that's true enough."

But then he stood abruptly and crossed over to a window, looking out on the patio. She followed behind him confused by the sudden shift in mood.

"What's the matter?" she asked.

"It's a bit more complicated here than you might think, Julia."

He seemed intensely caught up in his thoughts, so she waited patiently. "You see, while we were in 1910, there was a protection of sorts, although granted, Mr. Montamat did find a way to disrupt things. But here, well, he is on the same plateau. Any move we make, any paranormal activity, will be quite easy for him to trace."

She tried to soak in exactly what he was telling her. "That was why you brought me to 1910."

He stared at her intently, "One reason, one important reason, I thought we had a chance there to reach her outside of the grasp of anyone else."

"And here?" she asked.

He shook his head, "If we try anything now, if you do, Julia, it will draw him straight to us. I don't want to risk that. I can't risk you like that."

She shook her head, "But he has been near me, just yesterday."

"Yes, but he still doesn't know that you're lying to him, that you've aligned yourself with me."

She smiled a bit wryly, "Is that what you call it?"

He moved to her, taking her hand still as grave as ever. "The issue in the past was betrayal. Is that something you really want to stir up in him again?"

She shook her head, "I can't worry about him now. I won't be afraid of him."

He smiled, gently caressing her cheek with his hand. "Stubborn."

"You never told me what happened to him in that past life. He just got away with murder?"

A bit of the light left his eyes, "No, he didn't get away with it."

She looked at him questioningly, "What do you mean?"

"It was discovered rather quickly by his cousin."

"By you?"

"Yes."

"What did you do?"

His eyes seemed to glaze over a bit in a way that sent a chill of foreboding through her. "I reacted. There was a struggle, and then I killed him with his sword."

She felt stunned. She'd never had an inkling of that in her visions, but then again, she'd departed the scene by the time this took place. "You did?"

He continued to touch her, to lightly touch her hair. "You doubt it?"

"Doesn't that make things—"

"Complicated? Extraordinarily."

"And what happened to Antoine?"

Again, his expression was distant as though he was seeing her but also somewhere else. "From what I can gather he, or rather I, flung himself into the Mississippi in total devastation. Killing yourself in some circles is as destructive as killing another." He then focused on her again, "Past lives are complicated, Julia. They are us and yet not us. This is the only life you will live as who you are, your soul, but your spirit lives many times over."

She shook her head, "There is a difference between a spirit and a soul?"

He nodded, "Yes, the soul does the work for the spirit."

"The karma?"

"It's complicated."

She sighed, "So I gather. What are we going to do?"

"I imagine we're going to find the elemental. But it might be best to do it on foot, a bit less easy to trace."

"Just let me change."

And then, before she could move, he grasped both her arms with his hands unexpectedly. "In a little while," he nearly whispered, then gently but insistently pulled her in for a kiss. Again, her mind began to swirl, and her heart clutched in response, reminding her how deeply she had already fallen.

Revisiting Nicholas' Creole Cottage

Chapter Twenty-Seven

She brushed out her long brown hair, twisting it up into a soft bun just to get it off of her neck. "I've been thinking," he said.

She turned around. Nicholas was sitting on the edge of her bed. "Thinking what?" she smiled.

He held out his hand to her, and she took it, perching herself just beside him on the mattress they'd availed themselves of passionate use not so many minutes ago. "You should pack a bag."

Her eyes widened, "Why? Where am I going?"

He squeezed her hand, evidently deep in thought. "It would be safer at my place. Christian doesn't know it, and it's closer to the French Quarter."

"What do you mean? You have a place here?"

He looked at her a bit quizzically, "Yes, the house on Royal Street in the Faubourg Marigny."

"You mean that same house I—" her voice dropped off in astonishment.

He smiled, "Yes, I thought you liked it."

"So not the point. I don't understand how it's possible."

He was softly stroking a tendril of her hair while he elaborated, which actually made it more difficult to focus. "When you travel as I do, it helps to have a solid point of reference, like the house. I made arrangements in the past to make sure it stayed in my possession."

"But for some reason, I thought you hadn't been here very long."

"I haven't, not really. But I established a foothold here once I knew it was important. Time isn't nearly that fixed, unshakable thing everyone believes it is. It's actually extremely fluid."

"So, you changed things?"

He smiled, "Or perhaps made them exactly as they should be. "

"Not sure I understand, not entirely sure I want to."

He nodded, "Pack a bag. I'd like to keep my eye on you until we can settle things in some way."

"I have some deadlines. I'll have to bring my art supplies."

"No problem, there's plenty of room, no servants, just you and me."

She smiled, heading toward a hall closet where she kept her suitcase and art bag. Her stomach was filled with butterflies, good and bad ones. The last time she'd gone to stay at his mysterious cottage, it had not been her choice, but this time was something else. What did it mean, and where were they headed? In some ways, it felt like an exciting adventure, and in others, it felt as though her life was spinning out of her control, a terrifying prospect.

Nicholas wandered through Julia Moreau's house — his mind expanding, considering, and for the most part, just feeling. The time that had passed for him since her departure from his house in 1910 had been longer than it was here. It had been jarring and risky to use his skill to virtually fling her back to the very spot where he had taken her from. There were so many variables at play, among them a genuine possibility she would remember nothing of their time together, that she would simply slip back into her own life and forget that Nicholas Burke ever existed. The way things had shifted for him so quickly, he still found it unfathomable. Against all probabilities, against his plans, and to a degree against his will, he had fallen in love with the young woman he had dragged through time to help him on his quest.

Consequently, he'd spent the past week largely frustrated by his failure to cope with the elemental and extreme anxiety about Julia's well-being. Not only had he sent her away out of concern for her safety, but he'd also thrown her right back into the clutches of a man who had been absolutely ruthless and fatal to her in a former life. Needless to say, it wasn't his finest hour.

At least, some of it had been washed away when he returned to the present. He'd pulled up in front of her house and parked his car on the curb, entirely prepared to knock on her door and be greeted by a woman who had no clue who he was. But as soon as he'd stepped foot on the lawn, he'd felt a pull, and he followed it to a small metal gate that was easy enough to unlatch. As he walked around the side of the house, the pull became stronger, threads of energy guiding him to a lovely stone-laid patio and a fountain at its center. For some reason, it reminded him so strongly of the elemental, although there was, in reality, nothing of a resemblance between the two. It was such a hot day, but there was a coolness here, a comfort. And then his eyes drifted to the back of the house, a glass sunroom, where he saw her sitting behind an art table in deep concentration.

He allowed his mind to open to her, to try to feel if he was still there somewhere. And then, in response, her eyes lifted, meeting his. She stood up slowly and opened the door that led into the room. He didn't stop to think, to feel, to be sure. He moved on instinct, at a primal level, just needing her in his arms again — that contact that seemed to salve and heal all the blows the world continuously inflicted.

He was standing in her sunroom from the other side this time, staring outside at the patio, at the statue in the fountain again, wondering if his or, rather, their quest was already over, but they simply hadn't accepted it yet. He was at a loss as what to do. But Julia, and he couldn't help smiling, Julia was leading the charge now, not willing to accept defeat. So, they would try again, against all odds and against all logic, they would try again. He waited quietly with a calm mind and peaceful heart for the woman he loved.

She closed the small suitcase, surveying around her one last time to ensure she'd forgotten nothing. And then her eyes unexpectedly locked on the figure of her Aunt Lilia standing in the corner of the room, watching her calmly as though she'd been doing it for some time. Julia looked at her, smiling, "That's strange. I usually get some indication before you arrive."

"You're preoccupied," her aunt responded softly.

She focused on the figure before her, who she now recognized was wearing a very solemn expression. "What's the matter?" she asked.

Aunt Lilia drifted closer to the bed, standing in front of her. "You're sure of this, Julia? What you're doing?"

A tendril of concern swept across her formerly contented state. "What do you mean?"

"This path you're going down is not without its perils."

She turned back to her activity, zipping up the soft suitcase. "I know, but it's something I feel l must do."

"For him?" she asked.

Julia looked up into her aunt's placid features. There was very little hint of emotion there except in her eyes, her wide brown eyes so deep and laced with genuine concern. "You don't trust him?"

"It doesn't matter anymore what I think. You must listen closely to yourself. Of all things, you must acknowledge that lesson your life has taught you. You cannot ignore your feelings. They speak to you. They guide you. It is disastrous to repress them."

She stared at her aunt, feeling the truth in her words. So many times in the past, she would simply bury and dismiss what she was feeling in order to proceed with the things she felt she ought to do. It had been a calamitous mistake on her part — bringing more heartache and damage to her life than she could have ever foreseen. "I'm not doing that now," she spoke calmly and clearly in a voice she rather admired.

And then her aunt did something she rarely did. She smiled, albeit ever so slightly. "Then, I can only send you on, my dear, with my prayers and my love." Just before her aunt left, she heard almost the slightest murmur. "I'm proud of you, my child."

It felt odd traveling down Royal Street in Nicholas' black sedan. As they crossed Esplanade and headed into the Faubourg Marigny, she couldn't help but recall traveling the same street route with him in a horse-drawn carriage only days ago. He pulled the car into a driveway on the side of the house, which she did not remember being there before. The outside of the structure had been painted, although not in a shade so dissimilar from the one she remembered. He stopped the engine, then glanced at her speculatively. "All right?" he asked.

She smiled, "Feels very strange."

"Yes, well, stick around with me, and you'll get used to it." He stepped out of the car managing to make it around to the other side and open her door before she had a chance to. Again, she remembered him taking her hand, helping her out of the carriage in front of Josephine Delachaise's mansion.

Inside, the house felt curiously familiar and, for the most part, unchanged. As they walked into the front parlor or rather den now, she noticed some of the furniture she remembered wasn't there anymore, although a good part remained — after all, antiques often held up well. Nicholas, carrying her suitcase, led her through the rooms and back to the winding staircase to the second floor. As he opened her old bedroom, she was taken aback at how much it had altered. Instead of the huge brass bed in the center of the room, there was a smaller white wrought iron daybed against the wall, and all the original furniture had gone as well, now having shifted to a collection of white furniture — a dresser, nightstand, long mirror. "Wow, this is different," she couldn't help but express.

He smiled, seeming a bit distracted. "Yes, I'll just leave your things in here." The moment actually felt surprisingly awkward when she suddenly realized there was some question mark in the air as to where she'd be sleeping. Given their relationship over the past few days, it wasn't inconceivable this was actually them sort of moving in together. It was something she traditionally wasn't crazy about, though it was a popular social trend. Odd, with Nicholas, all the rules seemed to be thrown out the window, but given the gravity of what was going on, defining their relationship felt a bit secondary.

He looked at her with a change of expression. "Did you bring your insulin? I can put it in the refrigerator downstairs."

She nodded, feeling out of sorts in the whole situation. Clearly, every inch of this was new territory. "Oh, that would be great." She reached into her suitcase, pulled out a small bright purple bag filled with all her diabetes paraphernalia, and handed it to him.

He took the glittery purple bag, commenting lightly, "Very stylish."

She smiled a little sheepishly, "This all feels very weird to me."

"Yes, we're breaking new ground here. How about we meet downstairs once you've settled in, and we'll talk about strategy? A little unexpectedly, he kissed her quickly and then left the room. Yes, she'd told her aunt she was sure of what she was doing. But just now, all she felt was off-balance.

The Hunt for the Elemental

Chapter Twenty-Eight

Nicholas waited for Julia downstairs in the study. For the most part, the furnishings had been kept unchanged here, except for the sofa. The Chesterfield had been replaced by a modern leather sofa — one absence that, considering his fond memories, he regretted. It had been no easy feat keeping the house in his possession for over a hundred years. There had been several time jumps once he'd made plans to initially enlist Julia's aid. The first had been obtaining the house and establishing himself in the present. Time bending, he found, always required some stability of place. That was why it was easier to send Julia back to the point from which he'd taken her. For himself, he'd used this house as a touchstone from which to travel and establish a line of residence from the present backward. In 1910, he'd actually spent some six months there establishing himself, coordinating the purchase of the place and a solid deed as well as décor. It wasn't an inexpensive endeavor, but money was not a problem for him. Time bending had its side benefits as well.

But what he found interesting was the way things had shifted ever so subtlety. Pieces of furniture he hadn't originally placed in the house were here now — small changes. It wasn't a perfect mesh, but as the masters he had studied from explained to him through the years, time was not a solid thing. The past was still evolving, even as the present and future. It had taken his traditionally pragmatic mind a long time to grasp that concept, not a straight line but rather a bending river that intersects with itself at points.

And then his mind changed course, drifting back upstairs to Julia, seeming so shaken by being here again, how the ground had shifted between them since their initial meeting. Who had told him — *"Always expect the unexpected?"*

But he hadn't, hadn't even considered the possibility of what would evolve. Although, if he were honest with himself, it would have seemed a bit shocking. He couldn't have imagined that once he'd brought her here to this house, to the past, the impact she would have on him. He was not an engaging person. He deliberately held himself at a distance. In some ways, it was necessary for the kind of work he'd done, removing himself emotionally from people's lives in order to pragmatically evaluate them. But something about her was different, powerful, almost like a collision of energy when they met. It was a response he tried hard to bury but was intrigued by as well. There had been women in his life along the way, ones he worked with, some he was involved with, but nothing on this level. No matter what barriers he put up, she easily brushed them aside as though they were of no consequence. And then there was that night when he stopped burying everything, and everything had changed. But to what exactly, he asked himself. What exactly could he offer her? What sort of life would they build together once this was over, if this ever was over?

And then the energy shifted, and Julia walked into the room. She smiled and asked quietly, "Okay, where do we start?"

She was grateful she had brought a hat, a small white summery cap she used for such occasions. Nicholas had donned a khaki sort of flat cap that reminded her curiously of the past. Though, in general, even dressed in modern-day clothing, he reminded her of another time. She suspected that was because it was in the past where they'd begun their association and where she'd ostensibly fallen in love with him. But today was not the day to consider such personal things. They were on a hunt of sorts.

Although there was some shifting cloud cover overhead, in essence, it was hot, and they had set out on foot from Nicholas' cottage down Royal Street. "For some reason, I thought Benjamin Lamarque's house was on St. Charles like Josephine's."

He shook his head, "No, he lived deep in the French Quarter. Are you all right? Did you get enough to eat?"

"Yes," she answered, smiling as they continued the walk, not fast, not slow, just a brisk pace. They'd wiled away so much of the morning at her house before they'd returned to Royal Street. It was close to noon when they'd finally settled on their plans. But Nicholas had insisted they eat first, leaving her in the house to get ready and appearing shortly with po'boys he'd picked up from a nearby restaurant. They'd settled into his study, having lunch, strategizing, making her feel very at home and cozy. She'd often found older houses uncomfortable, too laden with baggage from other people's lives, but not Nicholas' house. Here, in her own time frame, she felt even more connected to it.

As they crossed Elysian Fields, Julia began to feel the familiar pound of the French Quarter approaching. Just getting closer to it shifted, almost thickened, the atmosphere a bit. She assumed it was the layers of history, activity, and living that were so densely packed in that relatively small perimeter.

There were so many different imprints of energy left from its varied, illustrious, and tumultuous past. As they approached, she slowed herself to open a bit to try to reach out for the vibrations of the elemental.

"Be careful," Nicholas murmured beside her. "You must be very controlled with everything. Only use your eyes and ears now. Otherwise, he'll pick up on you."

She nodded, now fully recognizing the precariousness of their endeavor. As they began the walk across Esplanade, she continued to be disturbed by what Nicholas had said. Amidst everything, she'd forgotten entirely that Christian Montamat was anywhere around or that he existed at all. It was a bit jarring for her to recall the potential complication he imposed on their actions.

Once past Esplanade, they continued on Royal Street, deeper into the Quarter. It wasn't the weekend, so it did not have the same frenetic quality. Things were quieter, also slower. Beside her, Nicholas seemed focused. Evidently, he knew exactly where he was headed. "How are we going to get in the house?" she asked, the potential problem suddenly dawning on her.

"Don't worry," he answered.

Finally abandoning Royal, they took a quick right onto St. Phillip Street. Here, it was a curious mix of houses, townhouses, and storefronts. As they slowed their pace, Julia felt a distinct pull of energy, strong enough that she didn't even have to attempt to track it. "Nicholas!"

He took her hand and squeezed it. "Try not to focus on it too much, Julia."

As they continued walking down a few blocks further, the landscape shifted with more private residences, or rather Creole Townhouses as her mother had termed them — great tall buildings decorated with a succession of wrought iron balconies. And then, almost abruptly, they stopped right in front of one that seemed to stretch up three stories. It was an off-white stucco, almost understated in its appearance, but she felt a rush of energy from it that made her dizzy. And then, as though without thought, Nicholas rang the doorbell. She looked at him curiously, wondering what particular strategy he had in mind. After waiting for scant moments, the door swung open, and they were greeted by an elderly woman with completely silver hair. She smiled broadly, "You must be Dr. Burke."

Nicholas smiled charmingly, "Yes, Mrs. Andrews, and this is my fiancée, Julia Moreau."

Julia's eyes widened in surprise at the identification, but Nicholas' gaze calmly met hers as though all was as it should be. With his hand at her back, Nicholas ushered her within to follow behind Mrs. Andrews through the foyer of what she assumed to be the former Lamarque home into a rather palatial living area. Still, in a bit of a swirl from the quick escalation of events, Julia was again struck by how deceptive these French Quarter homes were — often appearing subdued on the outside but hiding a remarkably opulent and lush interior. But of course, that was how the early Creoles had desired them to be, so far afield from modern standards, which demanded the luxury be readily apparent on the outside so that your neighbors could admire it. The delicate silver-haired lady led them to an antique sofa, strongly reminding her of the décor of Josephine Delachaise's home in 1910. Mrs. Andrews was dressed more formally than they were in an old-fashioned paisley print dress, which made Julia feel a bit out of place in the khakis she'd chosen for the jaunt. But then again, this was modern New Orleans, a place of mass contradiction. "I'm sorry. I expected my granddaughter to be here to join us. But you know, young people these days."

She perched herself on the edge of the pink sofa, Julia sat beside her, and Nicholas took a matching fauteuil chair on the other side of a long marble coffee table. "Would you like tea?" she asked a little blandly but amiably.

Julia smiled, then glanced at Nicholas while waiting for him to take the lead. After all, this was his contrivance. "No, thank you, we're fine. I appreciate you seeing us. As I told you on the phone, my father had an acquaintance with yours."

Mrs. Andrews nodded as Julia began to put the pieces together. Her father was Benjamin Lamarque. But she wondered, distracted, why the woman would allow them access to her home based on Nicholas' word of the connection. It seemed very odd, but then again, considering Nicholas' particular persuasive powers, it made sense. The elderly woman smiled, "What an interesting coincidence," she said graciously, then was silent, leaving an awkward space in the air.

"Your home is just lovely," Julia interjected.

"Oh, thank you," Mrs. Andrews responded. "It has been in the family well for over a hundred years. It belonged to my grandfather, and my father, Benjamin, inherited it upon his death."

"Yes, my father mentioned visiting this house and how impressed he was by the lovely courtyard. I don't suppose there is any way we could look at it?"

Again, there seemed to be an awkward moment as though Mrs. Andrews wasn't sure how to reply. "Well, I suppose, if you like." She rose and began to meander through the house slowly. Julia's eyes momentarily clashed with Nicholas' behind the elderly lady's back, but he held a finger up to his lips to motion her into silence — lovely. As they slowly wound through what she could only term as a small mansion, strange feelings tried to wrap around her—layers of upset, past and present. Clearly, no matter how long it had been in the family, this had not been a happy house.

Finally, they paused as they reached a room that seemed to be some sort of library opening with wide golden gilded, French doors out onto the patio. Mrs. Andrews just stood on the threshold, gesturing widely with her hands. "Do you mind if I don't join you? I can't take the heat these days."

Nicholas smiled graciously, "Of course," grasping Julia's hand and ushering her outside. It was a lovely place, with manicured rose beds, artfully placed foliage, and a series of levels or steps leading to the centerpiece of the large fountain in the middle of the yard. But as they approached, Nicholas stopped short rather quickly, and Julia immediately gleaned why. At its center was not the lovely woman in Grecian garb they'd expected but rather a delicate swan. "It's gone," she whispered.

And his grasp on her hand tightened, although he said nothing.

An Unexpected Confrontation

Chapter Twenty-Nine

Mrs. Andrews looked confused at the question as though in concentration. "You know, I vaguely remember such a statue, but I was so young it's hard to recall details."

Julia felt her heart picking up its beat in a mild panic. But Nicholas seemed focused, compelling in his manner. They were standing in the large library just inside from the patio. "I know it seems odd, Mrs. Andrews, but my grandfather was particular about mentioning that statue. It would be most helpful if you have any idea where it might be now."

The elderly woman frowned. It was clear that this visit and particular trip down memory lane was becoming more than a bit taxing for her. And then Nicholas did something that surprised even Julia. He unexpectedly reached out and grabbed Mrs. Andrews' hand. In that instant, Julia could feel a directed rush of energy from him to the daughter of Benjamin Lamarque. Mrs. Andrews' eyes widened with a startled expression and then softened almost immediately, looking a bit dazed as he coaxed her, "Think, go back."

There was just silence, and for a moment, Julia thought the elderly lady had lapsed into something akin to a trance, but then her voice came to them, although weakly. "My mother, my mother, Anne." A flash of the thin, frightened figure of young Anne Lamarque seared across Julia's memory. "She did it while he was away. I was a little girl, only five or six."

Mrs. Andrews leaned against the door frame as if she needed support, but Nicholas continued to hold her hand and lead her with his soothing yet insistent voice. "What happened?" he compelled.

"She had it taken away. It was important to my father, and she wanted—" her voice cracked and drifted off.

"She wanted what?" he continued to push.

Julia could feel a swirl of upset in the French Quarter mansion as if the walls were suddenly purging themselves of the past. She could feel Anne flying through the house in emotional tirades set off by anything. It was the stress, the stress, and all the energy he'd taken from her. It damaged her, made her mind weak, susceptible, and finally unbalanced.

"She was so angry all the time. I remember I would hide in my bedroom when she was having a spell. The statue," she hesitated.

"It's all right now, tell us." He pushed.

"The statue, sometimes he would just stand outside staring at it for hours, just mesmerized." She smiled, "He used to tell me it was really alive, some fairy creature that would escape at night and visit me in dreams. But my mother, it made her angry because it meant so much to him. So, one week, when he was away on a trip, she had it removed, sent away."

Julia glanced at Nicholas, but his entire focus was on Mrs. Andrews, "Where was it that she sent it, Amelia?"

The old woman's blue-gray eyes squinted, almost as though she were trying to see, as though memory had become visual for her. Then the tension left her face, and she relaxed in a smile. "It's all right, Amelia," she told me. "They will take care of her."

"They?" asked Nicholas.

And then she turned to him with a bright smile that gave Julia a glimpse of what she must have looked like as a young woman, "The nuns would take care of her, the Carmelites."

Nicholas' eyes widened, and he turned to Julia with question. "The Carmelites?" he asked.

"You mean on Rampart Street?"

Mrs. Andrews looked at her suddenly in confusion as though she had walked out of a fog. "I'm sorry. What were you saying, dear?"

As they walked out of Benjamin Lamarque's former residence on St. Philip Street, Nicholas began grilling her, "Who are the Carmelites?"

"I don't know that much. Historically, they were a very strict order of cloistered nuns. They used to have an extensive complex on Rampart Street but sold it in the early 70s. I think it's some sort of Catholic complex now."

She instinctively turned on St. Philip and headed up toward Rampart, but unexpectedly, Nicholas caught her arm. "No, let's go back and get the car. I have a feeling this isn't the end of it."

By the time they returned to the house on Royal Street, Julia could feel her head spinning. All her life, she'd found being a diabetic was always a balance between insulin, exercise, and eating — actually a bit of a tight-wire act. As they walked into the coolness of the front hallway, she felt Nicholas' hand on her arm. "Are you all right?" he asked. He could feel the change in her. She was sure of it. He'd become so attuned to her that she didn't even have to say anything.

"I think I need something. It seems to be a low blood sugar."

He led her to a chair just past the den's entrance. "I'll get you something," he said lightly, kissing her on the head before he disappeared down a hallway.

Julia eased back in the chair and closed her eyes for a moment. It was a peculiar onset, how quickly the hypoglycemic episode had swooped in. In a way, she supposed it made sense, the exercise, maybe even the stress, but traditionally, that would make her blood sugar go up, not down. But she breathed deeply and tried to steady herself. Everything, for a moment, seemed to swirl as she relaxed, and she recognized, perhaps a bit too late, that this wasn't a low blood sugar after all.

She opened her eyes groggily to a large, drafty room with a crackling fireplace on the other side of its highly polished wooden floor. Instinctively, she pulled a shawl lightly draped across her shoulders more tightly around herself. But then again, the long antebellum gown she wore covered her so completely, except her shoulders and arms, which, due to the provocative style of the dress, were quite exposed.

Of course, there was confusion in her mind, but again, her senses felt groggy, and she was not quite attached. "Don't fight it right now. It will only make it harder."

Her eyes focused on the author of the voice, a man she knew from somewhere. He had dark hair, nearly coal-colored, and a similar mustache against a rather pale face. She grimaced. With distraction, she realized this could be quite bad. He wore a white shirt, casually untucked, but an unusual one, more ruffled and definitely out of style, over navy blue, fitted trousers. "Julia," he began. "Forgive my impetuousness, but it was necessary I talk to you."

She tried to get up from the wingback chair, but her head swirled again, and she leaned back. This wasn't what happened with Nicholas, she realized with distraction. It was clear to her that she wasn't really here.

"Yes, you aren't physically here." Dismally, she connected with the fact that he was reading her thoughts. "You're not Philippe," she murmured, her voice sounding oddly drugged.

The man smiled broadly, "Well, yes and no, let's say predominantly no right now."

"Christian," she murmured. She was so sleepy. She felt herself just drifting away. "Are you planning to commit murder again?" she asked distantly, considering that this wasn't the safest route, but then again, she was pissed off. She was tired of being some sort of plaything to be yanked here and there at someone else's pleasure.

He frowned, "This isn't what this is about."

She put her hand up in front of her face so she could examine it. It was small, delicate, and yet weathered a bit. But it wasn't her hand. Clearly, she was borrowing the body of Ovelia. "Isn't it?" she murmured. "Because you've decided, so we're walking around in the bodies of our former selves, and you don't want to discuss the fact that you, in this incarnation, murdered your wife."

"We have all done things in past lives that we would not do again," he said with a certain degree of steel in his voice.

"Really? Well, yes, Nicholas told me that he killed you with your own sword. But we all know you had that coming."

"Enough, Julia." His voice snapped angrily.

This was good. Maybe—she wasn't sure—but keep dragging him off course. "Oh, is that how you handled Ovelia? Yelling at her when you didn't like something, then snapping her neck?"

It was clear she was reaching him or maybe reaching Philippe. His eyes looked absolutely enraged. Maybe he wasn't nearly in as much control of this as he wished. "This is about the elemental."

She straightened up in the uncomfortable chair as much as she could in her groggy state. "Really, is it? And how far do you go for that as well? Does someone have to die as they did here?"

"Stop it," he commanded loudly.

And Julia's eyes snapped open. She was once again in Nicholas' den, now staring into Nicholas' eyes. Her throat felt bone dry, but she was back, in her body, grounded again. "What happened?" she asked.

He held her arms with his hands, his expression marred with deep concern. "We don't have much time," he said. "Now, he knows what we know."

The Question of the Future

Chapter Thirty

Julia sat at a small metal breakfast table in the kitchen, silently munching on a piece of toast and peanut butter and drinking a cup of juice, although curiously enough, she didn't feel at all as though she needed it now. Clearly, she'd mislabeled what was happening to her as a hypoglycemic episode while it had been something else entirely. "I don't get it," she said to Nicholas' back. He was staring out one of the side windows of the kitchen, clearly in some sort of contemplation.

"Don't get what?" he asked, not turning around.

"How could he know everything now? I thought you put up some sort of psychic barriers."

"I did," he said, finally turning around. "But by taking you, or rather your spirit, to another place, he brought you outside of the barriers I'd created. Actually, quite creative, I have to give it to him."

Julia frowned, pushing away the unfinished snack, feeling filled to the max with toast and peanut butter. She glanced around the kitchen again. It was, in reality, the first time she'd seen it in either time frame. It was a nice little nook, predominantly pale yellow, not terribly large, but outfitted with modern appliances. For a second, she thought of Alice and her mother, Jessamine. "Well," she offered, "if you were unable to do anything with the elemental, it's unlikely he could."

"Maybe," he said a bit grimly. "But he could take it back to England, tap into its energy somehow without releasing it. There are all sorts of unpleasant possibilities. And then there will never be a chance."

Julia sighed deeply, "Maybe we should try to go to the Carmelite convent or, rather, the former Carmelite convent. How late is it?"

He glanced at his watch. "After four, it will have to keep until the morning. In any case, you might need to rest."

She shook her head, again feeling a pressing urgency from within. "But what if he gets there first?" she asked.

His looked at her with an unreadable expression. "I think she's safe for now. He couldn't take information from you that you didn't have."

"What do you mean?"

"You're assuming she's still on Rampart Street. Whereas, I am of the opinion that it's more than likely she is not."

"This has to stop," she remarked distractedly to Nicholas, who was intently flipping through a book on the desk in his study. He pulled off his reading glasses, which, for some reason, she found terribly sexy on him, and fully focused on her. She was standing on the other side of the room near the small fireplace that, given the peculiar New Orleans climate, hadn't been lit in ages.

"I know," he said quietly. "There is entirely too much risk to you."

She frowned, recognizing that they were definitely not on the same page. "That's not exactly what I meant. There must be a way to get him to back off."

"Only by ending it," he stated flatly. "But I would like to remove you from the mix."

She shook her head, "Then you'd have no hope."

He looked at her a bit quizzically. "How can you be so sure, Julia?"

It was a justified question. Why, indeed, was she so sure? "I don't know. But since he knows, as you said, what we know. Why don't we stop sneaking around?"

Nicholas eyed her with some intensity, walking across the room and taking her hand. "If we do that, Julia, it could become very risky."

She answered grimly, "It already is."

They'd had an early dinner at a small bistro just past Elysian Fields. It was a quiet dinner in the cozy little restaurant. Both of them were tired, too tired to keep up any kind of rambling conversation. So, instead, they simply enjoyed the same space where words weren't necessary. As they walked back to Nicholas' house, quietly ambling, it was possible to believe that their lives were simple and that the future stretched comfortingly before them, filled with the hope and possibility of any couple who had found each other. It was possible to believe that now, but a sense of foreboding muffled her simple dreams. In truth, nothing had ever been so complex.

"What if it works?"

"Hmm," he murmured as they slowly took a turn onto Royal Street.

"I mean, what will you do? Where will you go?"

"Oh, you mean, what does life look like beyond this?"

"I suppose something like that."

He shook his head. "Good question. I have a house up North in Massachusetts. That's where I was born. But I'm not particularly rooted. I've traveled so much."

"You have a house here," she murmured.

He squeezed her hand that he'd been holding. "I do. I know whatever happens, I'd like you with me, Julia."

She felt a flush sweep over her face at the somewhat unexpected pronouncement. "Are you sure about that? I mean, how would we work in a normal life?"

He laughed a bit spontaneously. "Well, I'm not sure if I could promise you a normal life. But when I introduced you to Mrs. Andrews as my fiancée, it felt natural and right."

He slipped his arm around her as they approached his house. It was lovely to look forward this way and honestly believe that everything might turn out how they wished. But, of course, deep down somewhere, the voice of cynicism and experience whispered to her, *"Now, honestly, when had that ever happened?"*

The Carmelite Convent

Chapter Thirty-One

Christian had been successful. After the episode at St. Louis Cathedral, he had suspected that Julia was not being honest with him and that somehow Dr. Nicholas Burke was in the mix here, orchestrating events. And so, he'd pulled the duplicitous Ms. Moreau back into the past they'd shared and virtually lifted the extraordinary details right out of her mind. It was quite simple now. All he had to do was head over to the former Carmelite convent and somehow obtain the statue that contained this being, this "elemental," as they had termed it. In fact, he was extraordinarily close to obtaining what he'd been after for so long.

He glanced around the long, cold room he'd remained in. Its walls were oppressive, exhaling the despair of so many lifetimes ago. There was no reason to stay here, none whatsoever. Ovelia, or rather Julia, had vanished. It was simply him now—him and Philippe staring into a long-ago crackling fireplace, burning, incinerating all that it touched. But his very limbs were filled with lead, and he couldn't make himself leave.

"And how far do you go for that as well? Does someone have to die as they did here?"

Ovelia, no, he meant Julia's cutting words continued to resound in his ears. This house they'd lived in was a cold house, but he'd made it a colder one. Indeed, how much did the ends justify the means? How far was he willing to go? And what would he lose in the bargain?

"All good questions," Gregory spoke from across the room. His monk's robes trailed across the highly polished floor as he made his way to Christian's side at the fireplace.

"I'm very close," he murmured.

"So, I see," Gregory smiled, pulling back the hood of his robe to reveal a finely sculptured face that Christian believed sometimes was just short of being angelic.

"You know, Nicholas Burke has no right to this." And his voice trailed off. He could hardly describe it as the Dubourg crystal anymore. Evidently, that was some sort of subterfuge.

Gregory softly patted his arm. "It's hard to cling to lies. Isn't it, my friend? No matter how comforting they may seem to us."

Christian strummed his fingers on the heavy cypress mantel. "I've come too far to let go of this," he said.

"This is a living entity you're battling for, Christian, one of God's creations, however extraordinary and unusual it may seem to us. There is no ownership here."

"But Burke wants—"

"To set is free. Not to profit, not to use," he pronounced softly. There was slight pain beginning to pound in his head that reminded him of Philippe — the life he had as Philippe and his crimes. "Yes, don't forget. Those that forget the past are doomed to repeat it."

Christian closed his eyes, allowing the searing truth of Gregory's words to soak in, and then his spirit returned to the present.

"Are you sure it's all right to do this?" she asked.

Nicholas paced across the small office at the end of the hall on the second floor. Julia had been surprised to find it virtually unchanged from her exposure to it in 1910 — the same comfortable chaise chair and roll-top walnut desk where Nicholas now sat. "It seems that any precautions we take, Mr. Montamat finds a way to breach, so speed is the only thing we have on our side now. I'll do my best to guard against interference. But you are the one who must make the journey."

"Exactly what sort of journey?" she asked as she leaned back and settled herself comfortably into the chaise lounge chair.

"This time, you must focus on your connection with the elemental and lock onto it completely." Julia closed her eyes. Her heart was beating madly now. They were going for broke here, and the possibility of their failure lying at her feet was petrifying. "Now follow my voice, Julia. Relax, relax completely."

She breathed in deeply. That was exactly what she needed, his voice lulling her into a quiet, meditative place. "Feel yourself letting go and opening to the vibrations around you." His voice was soft but so compelling, comforting. It was almost as though she could feel him in her mind now, speaking to her.

"How will I know?" she heard herself whisper, though somehow not actually voicing it physically.

"You must trust yourself. Trust your feelings completely."

So, she focused while at the same time allowing herself to let go of control. The air was thick with energy, but through it, she began to hear a sound—that distant strange buzzing sound she'd heard in her dream with Christian so long ago. And then she continued to let go, disconnecting from her earthly body, and began to be drawn to its source.

"It's all right, just follow it." Julia continued to hear Nicholas' voice guiding her in her mind. It comforted her to know now that wherever she traveled, he would be with her.

It was becoming louder, the buzzing sound. As she moved closer, it dawned on her that what she was actually hearing wasn't a buzzing at all but an energy vibration. The buzzing was only some sort of translation to earthly ears. This was how it manifested itself, this unique other-worldly vibration.

With one last conscious decision, she allowed herself to release completely and be drawn to the center.

And then suddenly, everything stopped. There was stillness as the air had shifted around her curiously. After what seemed to be several moments, Julia opened her eyes, although she could not now remember having closed them. Here, all around her, it was just dusk, and shadows had slipped randomly across the grounds. The sound of the water continued around her, the soothing sound of the water softly cascading down the sides of the statue — the statue of the Grecian girl that she remembered from Benjamin Lamarque's courtyard shone in the half-light. Finding her bearings, she slowly walked around the fountain, dimly recognizing that she was within the walls of the Carmelite convent as it had been. But immediately, she knew that something was off. This wasn't the present at all.

"No," a voice called to her from the shadows. And then a figure stepped into the receding light. It was a woman clothed in the white dress of a nun's garb, but with some confusion, she identified the face from long ago. She recognized her as young Anne Lamarque.

The moment seemed to stretch on forever as Julia tried to make some sense of what was happening. "I don't understand," she said softly. "You didn't become—"

Anne moved closer to her, "Become one of the Carmelite nuns?" She shook her head, "No, although my spirit needed a period of healing, and in odd moments, it was something I considered. No, Julia, nothing here is actual. It is representational."

"Symbolic?" Julia asked.

Anne smiled in a calm, relaxed way that Julia could not have imagined her doing during her difficult life. "In some ways, I am Anne, and I am the sisters who were here," she said, glancing up at the statue. It was glistening strangely in the semi-darkness, almost giving off its own luminescent glow. "And her as well. We are all here to set things right."

Julia waited, feeling an odd fluttering inside her. She couldn't feel Nicholas anymore, not at the moment.

"No, this is a place for females only tonight, Julia. It's important we make you understand. There is no need for power or control here. There is no ambition. We're all here now to nurture to heal."

"I don't understand," she said.

Anne answered quietly, "All of us have touched this lovely being in some way. When I was alive, I could feel her presence. She visited me in dreams, but I rejected her. I was so unhappy that this sort of pure light was intolerable to me." Now, she smiled sadly, "You see. I knew what I must do, what was right, but refused to do it."

Julia nodded, "You mean changing your life."

Anne smiled again, "You understand. My spirit wanted me to have the strength to leave, to live with purpose, to live the life I was meant to. But I was too weak to do it and having her near made my weakness more intolerable."

Julia carefully considered what had been said. "I see what you're saying. I think if I had stayed with my husband and gone on, I would have deteriorated as well."

Anne's blue eyes almost became brighter at Julia's words. "The sisters here took charge for a while. They didn't understand exactly what she was, but they could feel the energy, the purity. And—" then she stopped, seeming unwilling to voice it.

"When they left this place."

"Yes, when they left this place, she also left." She smiled a little sadly, and the intonation of her voice shifted ever so slightly. "You see. I remembered you and was always grateful for what you would do, Julia. I have learned from your world, watching, waiting, but it is important now that I return home." Julia felt a chill go through her, feeling the light coming from Anne's eyes now. She was no longer speaking to Anne or the nuns. In some way, it was her now, the elemental now communicating. "It must be your choice, of course. No one's life should be controlled by anyone else. Life is a gift."

She felt a fluttering in her chest, and her head swirled with the beautiful energy she remembered. The words softly whispered in the air as everything around her shifted: *"Your choice,"* and then Julia returned home.

The Choice

Chapter Thirty-Two

It was an overcast morning, which, considering the heat of New Orleans in August, was a blessing. They had parked Nicholas' car on the St. Charles Avenue side of Audubon Park and just began to walk.

The images of the night before floated into her mind: the journey to the Carmelite convent and her return home.

"And what did that mean, your choice?" Nicholas asked, a bit of concern on his face, his voice a tinge emphatic—demanding as he became when he knew things were out of his hands.

So, she'd quietly told him, "I'm not sure," a half-truth. It is an odd thing when decisions are already made. What a sense of peace it brings. But he was intuitive as well. He could sense the unknown lying at their feet, and for a man who was so powerful in his own right, it was difficult to relinquish control.

"All right, now we drop it. I have a very uneasy feeling about all of this."

But Julia had smiled and taken his hands in hers. "You know, I love you," she whispered.

His face registered some surprise, the gravity of what she'd said.

He'd kissed her intensely, passionately, and yes, a bit desperately. They'd spent the night together, and he'd told her many times over how much he loved her.

And this morning, when she'd explained that she believed she knew where the elemental was now, he'd looked surprised, indecisive. But a calm had come over her. *"It's your choice,"* the words continued to echo in her mind.

But then again, somehow, this choice felt as though it were made long ago.

As they slowly meandered through Audubon Park, they passed great, tall, towering trees, children playing, and young couples whispering to each other about their future. She felt a lightness as though the heartaches and misfortunes of her past were simply dropping away, as though she were shedding an old skin in preparation for becoming something else. Nicholas squeezed her hand, "We can go back," he told her.

But she turned to him and smiled. There was a building anticipation of seeing what was next.

A great cloudy sky stretched overhead, and she remembered things like sitting next to her mother as she painted and taking Nicholas' hand as she stepped out of a carriage — things that were golden, things that mattered.

They crossed roads and walked around the back of the long golf course, winding, turning in their journey. She wasn't entirely sure of where she was going, just continued to feel the source.

"What about Christian?" Nicholas asked, still beside her as she walked, but her mind felt the intense pull.

"He's gone now. He left this morning."

"He left? How do you know?" he asked, sounding a bit astonished.

She shook her head, "I could see it."

"There will be many things you will see," the air whispered around her.

It was odd, but now it didn't surprise her. She'd seen it before in passing—so many had—but she hadn't truly recognized it, not really until now. As they approached, she could see benches that had been put in around the circular platform. And she could hear the energy reverberating through the trees around them, a quiet hum, nearly musical, nearly a soft musical note.

Nicholas stopped outside the wide, circular platform with several steps leading up to the fountain. "Good God," he said in disbelief. "Are you telling me it's been here all this time just like this?"

Julia took in the vision of the Grecian statue, her arms delicately stretched upward as they had been the night before. She could hear her soft whispers in the breeze around them.

Nicholas was beside her, his hands grasping her arms. "I don't understand, Julia. What is it?"

"Hide in plain sight," she murmured. "The Carmelites donated her to the city once they'd left. You see, she knew me from the very beginning. That was the connection. She remembered."

"Remembered what?" he asked, still with a bit of confusion in his voice.

She could see the energy flowing outward and the connection being forged. "She remembered the future."

"What does that mean the future?"

She smiled at him, lightly putting her hand on his. "It's all right." And then she pulled away from him, walking up the steps, stepping into the wide pool of water. "My choice," she whispered, placing her hands on the statue and feeling the final step as the elemental merged into her.

The world swirled for a moment, and she felt a surge of gratefulness as the entity settled quietly into its long sleep.

In just seconds, Nicholas was behind her, plunging into the pool and wrapping his arms around her. "Julia, what have you done?" he asked in a panicked voice.

She breathed deeply as the energy within and around her settled — pure light, pure healing throughout her. And vision finally normalized again. "She's sleeping," she said quietly. "Preparing for the journey home. She'll do this for all my days on this earth, and when my spirit leaves this body, she will leave as well, finally able to return to where she belongs."

He was breathing deeply, almost as though he were in shock. "How could you do this?"

She wrapped her arms around him as well. "It's all right. All my life was leading to this. It was what I was meant to do."

The stillness wrapped around them, and a sense of peace flowed through Julia. The beautiful statue in the park was just that now—a statue, no longer a prison for something not meant for this earth. They walked out of the fountain, stepping back onto dry steps and back down to the ground. Julia's mind still swirled in dizziness with the energy the elemental had brought to her in the transference.

He kissed her cheek. "I love you," he whispered in a somewhat ragged voice.

She smiled, "In a way, I believe she has always loved you as well, Nicholas. Perhaps that was what drew her to earth."

"Let's go home," he said, wrapping his arm around her and pulling her close.

And slowly, still dripping with water, they began the slow walk back. *"There are many gifts,"* she could hear the whispers. But she would tell him later as she watched the clouds overhead begin to part.

"I would give gladly all the hundreds of years that I have to live, to be a human being only for one day, and to have the hope of knowing the happiness of that glorious world above the stars."— Hans Christian Anderson's The Little Mermaid

Finis

The Lady in the Blue Dress
6 x 9 Softcover & Hardcover 214 pages
ISBN 978-1-61342-600-5
ISBN (Hardcover) 978-1-61342-418-6

When she was a child, Mika Devalieur was introduced to her grandmother's most precious possession — a priceless and mysterious painting that she simply called The Lady in the Blue Dress. Upon Adele St. Clair's death, the painting is left in the care of her granddaughter with only one stipulation. Mika must hand over the family heirloom to a total stranger. Mika Devalieur desperately wants to deny her beloved grandmother's last request, but she can't. Torn between her Gran's last wishes and her desire to hold onto the Lady, she ultimately journeys to rural Virginia, where an enigmatic man shows her that this painting is only the beginning.

What quickly becomes clear is that James Clairmont knows much more about her and the Lady than he is letting on. He begins to slowly unravel a powerful supernatural connection that spans three generations of her family. Mika finds herself desperate to uncover the entire truth before she falls in love with a man filled with so many secrets — secrets about him, about her, and most especially about The Lady in the Blue Dress. (First published on Kindle Vella, episodes 1-23.)

Dumaine Street
6 x 9 Softcover & Hardcover 306 pages
ISBN 978-1-61342-902-0
ISBN (Hardcover) 978-1-61342-416-2

Voices in her head, catastrophic emotions, hallucinations — Rebecca Wells is more than convinced that she is losing her mind. And as a last-ditch effort, she contacts a self-professed counselor who seems convinced he can help.

Gabriel Sutton has abandoned the world of medicine to navigate a realm filled with psychic phenomena. Diagnosing Becca with extreme empathic abilities, he struggles to help her stabilize her gifts while trying desperately not to fall in love with his patient.

From the realm of vulnerability into a crusade to use their profound gifts to rescue others from peril on the other side of death, these two follow an astonishing and unpredictable path into each other's hearts.

The Tethering
A Portent of Crows
6 x 9 Softcover & Hardcover 201 pages
ISBN 978-1-61342-599-2
ISBN (Hardcover) 978-1-61342-419-3

Deborah Brandt's beloved Aunt Gena always told her that she was special, a bit different, and would have to live her life, unlike other people. Of course, this she disregarded as the ramblings of her lovely but notably eccentric aunt. Although there were the things that Aunt Gena said that seemed true — like Deborah being sensitive to energy shifts, having potentially psychic impressions, and dreaming of a spirit guide — none of it could be real. But the most ridiculous thing that her Aunt Gena told her before she died was that someone special was out there for her. She said that he was an extraordinary man who was not only her perfect match but someone who she would learn from so that they could help the world in difficult times. How ridiculous! It sounds like a fairy tale, and no such person exists.

Daniel Wren is unique. He has been raised and trained from a young age to hone his psychic gifts. He lives in a world unimagined by most. And he has been waiting for years to contact his counterpart, soulmate, if you will. But the problem is that she is painfully unaware of the type of life that he lives and the life she would be entering into if they came together.

His dilemma becomes how best to proceed. How can he win her over and move forward before outside forces take that decision away from him?

Travels into the Breach
Accounts of a Reluctant Mystic
6 x 9 Softcover & Hardcover 171 pages
ISBN 978-1-61342-323-3
ISBN (Hardcover) 978-1-61342-417-9

At first glance, his life seems quiet, serene, and even uneventful. Malachi McKellan, a 65-year-old widower and author of esoteric books, lives largely as a recluse in a house situated just off the banks of Bayou St. John in New Orleans. But unbeknownst to most, he is also a bit of a detective, a specific kind of detective whose specialty is psychic attacks. Alongside his lifelong companion and spirit guide Simon Tull, a 19th-century, 20-something English gent, Malachi battles the unseen, and is an unacknowledged hero to the most vulnerable. Most of the population have no idea what is really happening beneath the surface of the world in which they live.

In this collection of adventures, Malachi McKellan and Simon Tull wage war against the most insidious elements of the paranormal. In *The Three*, Malachi and Simon come to the aid of a young woman being victimized by a group of dark witches. An old apartment building is the scene of an unimaginable battle against monstrous forces in *The Lost Soul*. Malachi and Simon find themselves strategizing against a psychic vampire in *Obsession*, and *The Hotel* turns back time to the 1980s where Malachi confronts a demonic spirit. In *Between*, a past life is revisited as Malachi attempts to rescue a beloved sister from committing her existence to vengeance, and *The Wedding* takes a personal turn when Malachi must confront painful truths while endeavoring to protect his niece from a potentially devastating union.

Travel into the breach with a pair of paranormal warriors who choose to confront overwhelming forces on a battlefield unsuspected by most.

Gravier's Bookshop
A *New Orleans Paranormal Mystery* (#1)
6 x 9 Softcover & Hardcover 172 pages
ISBN 978-1-61342-288-5
ISBN (Hardcover) 978-1-61342-411-7

Max Gravier had no intention of becoming a recluse, but after his wife's death it seems his life is heading in that direction. He spends his time running Gravier's Bookshop on Magazine Street and occasionally on the quiet helps the police solve a crime with his psychic sensitivities. That is until he answers Caroline Breslin's call, a cry for help out of his dreams that draws him into a fierce battle for a young woman's soul.

In this first installment of The New Orleans Paranormal Mystery series, Caroline Breslin, an amazingly gifted empath, is determined to strike out on her own and has moved out from the protection of her family home. All is going extremely well until, of course, she comes under siege from a devastating supernatural attack. The last thing Caroline wants is to run back to her family for help, even though she is painfully in over her head. What she really needs is a knight in shining armor — or maybe just that guy that keeps haunting her dreams.

Join them and the whole Breslin family psychic clan in this first installment of The New Orleans Paranormal Mystery Series where you'll travel into a new world just a few steps into the turbulent realm of the unseen.

The Hotel Mandolin
A *New Orleans Paranormal Mystery* (#2)
6 x 9 Softcover & Hardcover 146 pages
ISBN 978-1-61342-290-8
ISBN (Hardcover) 978-1-61342-412-4

Peril is wrapped up in the most enticing of disguises in *The Hotel Mandolin*, the second installment of The New Orleans Paranormal

Mystery series. It's opulent, classic, and one of the most renowned hotels nestled deep in New Orleans' famous business district, but something is amiss at The Hotel Mandolin.

PI Peter Norfleet is calling out the big guns to help him investigate a recent suicide at the famous establishment — his good friend Max Gravier, a formidable psychic, and his girlfriend, Caroline Breslin, a talented empath. But none of them can seem to scratch the surface of this puzzle, no one except Cassie Breslin, Caroline's clairvoyant mother, who has somehow tapped into an unexpected connection with a tragic ghost from the turn of the century. And the more she uncovers, the more dangerous and malevolent the mystery becomes

The House at Pritchard Place
A *New Orleans Paranormal Mystery* (#3)
6 x 9 Softcover & Hardcover 138 pages
ISBN 978-1-61342-292-2
ISBN (Hardcover) 978-1-61342-413-1

Nothing is really wrong with the old Warrick House on Dante St. except that there most certainly is. Nothing is exactly wrong with its new mysterious owner except that Elise is sure that something doesn't add up. It isn't obvious, but sometimes the most dangerous things aren't.

In the third installment of The New Orleans Paranormal Mystery series, with the help of her very psychic sister and her children, the Breslin clan, Elise Ashford is about to embark on a wild rescue mission straight into another dimension that will land her squarely somewhere she doesn't expect, right back into her past. She'll land full circle; in a childhood home whose memory still haunts her to this day -- *The House at Pritchard Place*.

Sanctuary of Echoes
6 x 9 Softcover & Hardcover 371 pages
ISBN 978-1-61342-211-3
ISBN (Hardcover) 978-1-61342-409-4

Ghosts unacknowledged do not sleep.

Corey Knight has resigned herself to a quiet, reclusive life spent living out the rest of her days in her childhood home on the fringes of New Orleans' French Quarter. But the unexpected specter of her deceased father plunges her into a mad quest for a missing supernatural weapon unearthed long ago. And unfortunately, her only ally is a lost love she once betrayed.

Iain Shaw returns to New Orleans, a city he abandoned a decade before while fleeing a devastating past. Here, he is forced to confront it again in the visage of the woman he once adored - one that he is now determined to get back at any cost.

Follow them both in a wild paranormal tale of discovery and redemption as they confront and unearth the echoes of a buried and unyielding truth that once tore them irreparably apart.

A Quiet Moment
6 x 9 Softcover & Hardcover 273 pages
ISBN 978-1-61342-326-4
ISBN (Hardcover) 978-1-61342-435-3

Jacob Wyss is caught in a rut, in fact on the verge of being engulfed by it. After an excruciating and disillusioning divorce, his life as an artist in a sleepy-college town at the foot of the Appalachian Mountains has become quiet, routine, and maddening in its predictability. One wintry day, his deep restlessness drives him out in precarious conditions to a largely empty bookstore nearly devoid of another living soul, nearly.

Aimee Marston isn't like everyone else. On the surface, she lives a sedate life working as a feature writer for a small local newspaper in addition to several other editorial jobs to help make ends meet.

But just beneath, her existence is largely not her own. She is a sensitive, an empathetic psychic, guided by her calling to use her gifts to help others. Unfortunately, as a result, her secretiveness has made her defensive, protective of herself, and prevented her from having much of a life.

A psychic call for help sends Aimee out on a freezing January morning where her destiny and Jacob's collide sending both their lives spiraling onto an unexpected and often disturbing track. Two lonely souls connect, not by accident, but by design. Theirs is the intersection of two spiritual paths, two lovers who must struggle to overcome the phantoms of a past life, as well as the challenges of their own inner demons to carve out an extraordinary future together.

A Ghost of a Chance
6 x 9 Softcover 195 pages
ISBN 978-1-61342-162-8

You never know what's coming next.

Jack Brennan, an ambitious high-powered attorney, dies. But that's not the end, rather only the beginning. He finds himself constrained to an inexplicable afterlife as an earth-bound spirit trapped in an old Virginia farmhouse. His only companion is a very much living, reclusive writer of campy vampire novels. The maddening problem is that Hallie does not know he is there, nor that he is somewhat reluctantly falling in love with her.

Hallie Barkly is recovering from a painful and disillusioning divorce. Out of the ashes of her former life, she has managed to somehow forge a career and exorcise her demons by writing under the pseudonym of Sebastian Winters. Slowly, she is awakening to the fact that she is not alone.

Their lives intersect, and two unconventional lovers are brought together under insurmountable circumstances. Together they must battle an unseen force hell-bent on possessing Hallie's life and bridge death itself to make possible what cannot be — to find a chance.

Dragonflies - Journeys into the Paranormal
6 x 9 Softcover & Hardcover 176 pages
ISBN 978-1-88756-072-6
ISBN (Hardcover) 979-8-32548-418-6

In every form of creation, there is a blueprint for living, for experience, for interpretation. In flight, they can twist, turn, alter direction, pause in midair, and even fly backward. The dragonfly is the master of adaptability. They are a living prism, refracting light, and color, seemingly shifting their essence.

The lesson the dragonfly gives is that life is never what it appears to be.

In "The Wizard," as a novice practitioner of magic, Aurora Finn finds herself battling against the illusions of a powerful wizard intent on separating her from the world she knows. "The Sojourners" is a gentle story of a mother and daughter whose tenancy in an old Virginia farmhouse uncovers the trials and sorrows of its former occupants. A bookstore clerk gets an extraordinary customer on Halloween night in "Late One Night at Berstrums Books." In "The Tear," a woman coping with her fatal illness unknowingly begins a track on a mystical journey that will entirely restructure her vision of the world.

These stories follow the path of the dragonfly imbued with the momentum and energy of change, taking a winding and treacherous journey that ultimately leads to truth buried beneath perception.

Breaking Through the Pale
6 x 9 Softcover 134 pages
ISBN 978-1-88756-045-0

Journey with metaphysical author Evelyn Klebert into a collection of short stories that travel beyond the pale into the unpredictable realm of the paranormal.

In "A Grey Mourning," a disillusioned man encounters a mysterious being on the foggy streets of New Orleans. "Contact" is a tale of automatic writing, when a young artist establishes communication with a spirit guide, and the victim of a car crash unravels the true nature of her existence in "Dancing on the Threshold." The final tale is called "Isolation," in which a confused and disoriented woman finds herself in an old, quaint house where she must piece together the mystical implications surrounding her predicament.

Explanations
6 x 9 Softcover 82 pages
ISBN 978-1-93493-515-6

In this, her second poetry collection, Evelyn Klebert takes us down the intricate path of a personal journey. Life with its particular struggles, pitfalls, and ultimately triumphs clearly begins to mirror a universal path, the quest for answers that we all ultimately pursue. In this reflective, esoteric collection we can all explore and seek some of life's elemental mysteries and hopefully when all is said and done emerge with some *Explanations*.

The Witches' Own
6 x 9 Softcover & Hardcover 140 pages
ISBN 978-1-61342-058-4
ISBN (Hardcover) 978-1-61342-428-5

On the surface things seem quiet and serene in the picturesque coastal village of Kilmarnock, Virginia. But something unseen roams its lush forests as the past and present collide and the unthinkable begins to wreak its vengeance. Young Lucy Bonner is executed for witchcraft in the town's distant and brutal past. Her death triggers an unholy chain of events which grasp at the restless heart of novelist Peter McQuade, spurring him towards a quest to uncover the dark and terrifying truth.

The Left Palm
And Other Halloween Tales of the Supernatural
6 x 9 Softcover 117 pages
ISBN 978-1-93493-556-9

Halloween is the time of year when that veil between worlds is thinned, and you can just catch a quick glimpse into the realm of the unknowable. In this collection of short stories, Evelyn Klebert takes you to a place where ordinary life splinters into the sphere of the paranormal.

The journey begins with one woman's unstoppable quest for vengeance against a supernatural creature in "Wolves" and continues in an old historical graveyard where a horrifying discovery is uncovered in "Emma Fallon." In "The Soul Shredder," a psychiatrist's unusual patient opens his eyes to a disturbing new view of reality, while in "Wildflowers," a woman strikes up a supernatural friendship with impossible implications. And in "The Left Palm," a fortuneteller in the French Quarter receives a most unexpected and terrifying customer.

White Harbor Road
And Other Tales of Paranormal Romance
6 x 9 Softcover 130 pages
ISBN 978-1-61342-066-9

A psychic soul mate, a time traveler, a horror writer, and an enigmatic stranger take a selection of resilient, life-battered heroines to a place of paranormal healing and transformation. In this collection of short stories, *White Harbor Road* is the last stop where life's burdens and hardships evolve into something unexpected.

The Broken Vow
Vol. I of The Clandestine Exploits of a Werewolf
6 x 9 Softcover & Hardcover 204 pages
ISBN 978-1-61342-133-8
ISBN (Hardcover) 978-1-61342-420-9

In the heart of every man there is a history. In the heart of every monster there is a story. In this first installment of *The Clandestine Exploits of a Werewolf,* Ethan Garraint is on a vendetta that begins in the heart of the Pyrenees with the fall of Montségur and leads him to the streets of New Orleans nearly five hundred years later. But the person he chases isn't really a man anymore and Ethan has been a werewolf for almost a millennium. With the aid of a gifted seer, he is on a blood hunt that will culminate in a journey that crosses the line between heaven and earth and ends somewhere in between.

Considerations
6 x 9 Softcover 68 pages
ISBN 978-1-88756-062-7

Sometimes the struggle to understand the meaning and complexities of living comes down to a single moment of introspection or a fleeting yet meaningful reflection. This collection of poetry by Evelyn Klebert takes you down a winding path of self-discovery where the resolution may not always be absolute, but the journey is indeed unforgettable. It a wide and varied map of inspired poetry for your examination and consideration.

Appointment with the Unknown
The Hotel Stories
6 x 9 Softcover & Hardcover 155 pages
ISBN 978-1-61342-360-8
ISBN (Hardcover) 978-1-61342-421-6

A hotel, for most, represents a normal place, a predictable realm of commonality. One might even go as far to say a safe space, the reliable where nothing particularly unusual is expected to happen. Or is it? Dimensional traveling, spirit guides, mystical storms, and soul mates separated by time are only a few elements dotting this supernatural landscape. Drop into a collection of romantic paranormal stories where that place of commonality is only the threshold, the jumping-off point, for extraordinary adventures into the unknown.

Visit Evelyn's website at:
www.evelynklebert.com

Cornerstone Book Publishers
www.cornerstonepublishers.com